J. G. Ballard was born in 1930
his father was a businessman.
Harbor, Ballard and his family
prison camp. They returned to E
years at Cambridge, where he
worked as a copywriter and Cov
going to Canada with the RAF. In 1956 his first short story
was published in *New Worlds* and he took a full-time job on
a technical journal, moving on to become assistant editor
of a scientific journal, where he stayed until 1961. His first
novel, *The Drowned World*, was written in the same year.

His novel *Empire of the Sun* won the Guardian Fiction
Prize and the James Tait Black Award, and was filmed by
Steven Spielberg.

By the same author

NOVELS

The Drowned World
The Drought
The Crystal World
The Wind From Nowhere
Crash
Concrete Island
High-Rise
The Unlimited Dream Company
Hello America
Empire of the Sun
The Day of Creation
The Kindness of Women

SHORT STORIES

The Voices of Time
The Terminal Beach
The Day of Forever
The Disaster Area
The Overloaded Man
The Venus Hunters
The Atrocity Exhibition
Vermilion Sands
Low-Flying Aircraft
War Fever

J. G. BALLARD

Myths of the Near Future

Triad Paladin
GraftonBooks
A Division of HarperCollinsPublishers

Triad/Paladin
An Imprint of GraftonBooks
A Division of HarperCollins*Publishers*
77-85 Fulham Palace Road,
Hammersmith, London W6 8JB

Triad Paperbacks Ltd is an imprint
of Chatto, Bodley Head & Jonathan Cape Ltd
and GraftonBooks, A Division of HarperCollins*Publishers*

Published by Triad/Paladin 1984
9 8 7 6 5 4 3

First published in Great Britain by
Jonathan Cape Ltd 1982

ISBN 0-586-09112-2

Printed in Great Britain by
HarperCollinsManufacturing Glasgow

Set in Garamond

Contents

Myths of the Near Future

At dusk Sheppard was still sitting in the cockpit of the stranded aircraft, unconcerned by the evening tide that advanced towards him across the beach. Already the first waves had reached the wheels of the Cessna, kicking spurs of spray against the fuselage. Tirelessly, the dark night-water sluiced its luminous foam at the Florida shoreline, as if trying to rouse the spectral tenants of the abandoned bars and motels.

But Sheppard sat calmly at the controls, thinking of his dead wife and all the drained swimming-pools of Cocoa Beach, and of the strange nightclub he had glimpsed that afternoon through the forest canopy now covering the old Space Centre. Part Las Vegas casino with its flamboyant neon façade, and part Petit Trianon – a graceful classical pediment carried the chromium roof – it had suddenly materialized among the palms and tropical oaks, more unreal than any film set. As Sheppard soared past, only fifty feet above its mirrored roof, he had almost expected to see Marie Antoinette herself, in a Golden Nugget get-up, playing the milkmaid to an audience of uneasy alligators.

Before their divorce, oddly enough, Elaine had always enjoyed their weekend expeditions from Toronto to Algonquin Park, proudly roughing the wilderness in the high-chrome luxury of their Airstream trailer, as incongruous among the pine cones and silver birch as this latter-day

7

fragment of a neon Versailles. All the same, the sight of the bizarre nightclub hidden deep in the Cape Kennedy forests, and the curious behaviour of its tenants, convinced Sheppard that Elaine was still alive, and very probably held prisoner by Philip Martinsen. The chromium nightclub, presumably built thirty years earlier by some classically minded Disneyland executive, would appeal to the young neurosurgeon's sense of the absurd, a suitably garish climax to the unhappy events that had brought them together in the sombre forests of the Florida peninsula.

However, Martinsen was devious enough to have picked the nightclub deliberately, part of his elaborate attempt to lure Sheppard into the open air. For weeks now he had been hanging around the deserted motels in Cocoa Beach, flying his kites and gliders, eager to talk to Sheppard but nervous of approaching the older man. From the safety of his dark-ened bedroom at the Starlight Motel — a huddle of dusty cabins on the coast road — Sheppard watched him through a crack in the double blinds. Every day Martinsen waited for Sheppard to appear, but was always careful to keep a drained swimming-pool between them.

At first the young doctor's obsession with birds had irri-tated Sheppard — everything from the papier-mâché condor-kites hanging like corpses above the motel to endless Picasso doves chalked on the cabin doors while Sheppard slept. Even now, as he sat on the beach in the wave-washed Cessna, he could see the snake-headed profile cut in the wet sand, part of an enormous Aztec bird across which he had landed an hour earlier.

The birds... Elaine had referred to them in the last of her Florida letters, but those were creatures who soared inside her own head, far more exotic than anything a neurosur-geon could devise, feathered and jewelled chimeras from the paradises of Gustave Moreau. None the less, Sheppard had finally taken the bait, accepting that Martinsen wanted to talk to him, and on his own terms. He forced himself from

8

the motel, hiding behind the largest sunglasses he could find among the hundreds that littered the floor of the swimming-pool, and drove to the light airfield at Titusville. For an hour he flew the rented Cessna across the forest canopy, searching the whole of Cape Kennedy for any sign of Martinsen and his kites.

Tempted to turn back, he soared to and fro above the abandoned space grounds, unsettling though they were, with their immense runways leading to no conceivable sky, and the rusting gantries like so many deaths propped up in their tattered coffins. Here at Cape Kennedy a small part of space had died. A rich emerald light glowed through the forest, as if from a huge lantern lit at the heart of the Space Centre. This resonant halo, perhaps the phosphorescence of some unusual fungi on the leaves and branches, was spreading outwards and already had reached the northern streets of Cocoa Beach and crossed the Indian River to Titusville. Even the ramshackle stores and houses vibrated in the same overlit way.

Around him the bright winds were like the open jaws of a crystal bird, the light flashing between its teeth. Sheppard clung to the safety of the jungle canopy, banking the Cessna among the huge flocks of flamingos and orioles that scattered out of his way. In Titusville a government patrol car moved down one of the few stretches of clear road, but no one else was tempted out of doors, the few inhabitants resting in their bedrooms as the forest climbed the Florida peninsula and closed around them.

Then, almost in the shadow of the Apollo 12 gantry, Sheppard had seen the nightclub. Startled by its neon façade, he stalled the Cessna. The wheels rattled the palm fronds as he throttled up a saving burst of speed and began a second circuit. The nightclub sat in a forest clearing beside a shallow inlet of the Banana River, near a crumbling camera blockhouse at the end of a concrete runway. The jungle pressed towards the nightclub on three sides, a gaudy aviary

9

of parakeets and macaws, some long-vanished tycoon's weekend paradise.

As the birds hurtled past the windshield, Sheppard saw two figures running towards the forest, a bald-headed woman in the grey shroud of a hospital gown followed by a familiar dark-faced man with the firm step of a warder at a private prison. Despite her age, the woman fled lightly along the ground and seemed almost to be trying to fly. Confused by the noise of the Cessna, her white hands waved a distraught semaphore at the startled macaws, as if hoping to borrow their lurid plumage to cover her bare scalp.

Trying to recognize his wife in this deranged figure, Sheppard turned away for another circuit, and lost his bearings among the maze of inlets and concrete causeways that lay beneath the forest canopy. When he again picked out the nightclub he throttled back and soared in above the trees, only to find his glide-path blocked by a man-powered aircraft that had lifted into the air from the forest clearing.

Twice the size of the Cessna, this creaking cat's cradle of plastic film and piano wire wavered to left and right in front of Sheppard, doing its best to distract him. Dazzled by his own propeller, Sheppard banked and overflew the glider, and caught a last glimpse of the dark-bearded Martinsen pedalling intently inside his transparent envelope, a desperate fish hung from the sky. Then the waiting bough of a forest oak clipped the Cessna as it overran its own slipstream. The sharp antlers stripped the fabric from the starboard wing and tore off the passenger door. Stunned by the roaring air, Sheppard limped the craft back to Cocoa Beach, and brought it down to a heavy landing on the wet sand within the diagram of the immense beaked raptor which Martinsen had carved for him that morning.

Waves washed into the open cabin of the Cessna, flicking a cold foam at Sheppard's ankles. Headlamps approached along the beach, and a government jeep raced down to the water's edge a hundred yards from the aircraft. The young driver stood against the windshield, shouting at Sheppard over her headlamps.

Sheppard released the harness, still reluctant to leave the Cessna. The night had come in from the sea, and now covered the shabby coastal town, but everything was still lit by that same luminescence he had glimpsed from the air, a flood of photons released from the pavilion in the forest where his wife was held prisoner. The waves that washed the propeller of the Cessna, the empty bars and motels along the beach, and the silent gantries of the Space Centre were decorated with millions of miniature lights, lode-points that marked the profiles of a new realm waiting to reconstitute itself around him. Thinking of the nightclub, Sheppard stared into the firefly darkness that enveloped Cape Kennedy. Already he suspected that this was a first glimpse of a small corner of the magnetic city, a suburb of the world beyond time that lay around and within him.

Holding its image to his mind, he forced the door against the flood and jumped down into the waist-deep water as the last of the night came in on the waves. In the glare of the jeep's headlamps he felt Anne Godwin's angry hands on his shoulders, and fell headlong into the water. Skirt floating around her hips, she pulled him like a drowned pilot on to the beach and held him to the warm sand as the sea rushed into the silver gullies of the great bird whose wings embraced them.

Yet, for all the confusions of the flight, at least he had been able to go outside. Three months earlier, when Sheppard arrived at Cocoa Beach, he had broken into the first motel he could find and locked himself for ever into the safety of a darkened bedroom. The journey from Toronto had been a succession of nightmare way-stations, long delays in semi-derelict bus depots and car-rental offices, queasy taxi-rides slumped in the rear seat behind two pairs of dark glasses, coat pulled over his head like a Victorian photographer nervous of his own lens. As he moved south into the steeper sunlight the landscapes of New Jersey, Virginia and the Carolinas seemed both lurid and opaque, the half-empty towns and uncrowded highways perceived on a pair of raw retinas inflamed by LSD. At times he seemed to be looking at the interior of the sun from a precarious gondola suspended at its core, through an air like fire-glass that might melt the dusty windows of his taxi.

Even Toronto, and his rapid decline after the divorce from Elaine, had not warned him of the real extent of his retreat behind his own nerve-endings. Surrounded by the deserted city, it surprised Sheppard that he was one of the last to be affected, this outwardly cool architect who concealed what was in fact a powerful empathy for other people's psychological ills. A secretary's headache would send him on a restless tour of the design offices. Often he felt that he himself had invented the dying world around him.

It was now twenty years since the earliest symptoms of this strange malaise – the so-called 'space sickness' – had made their appearance. At first touching only a small minority of the population, it took root like a lingering disease in the interstices of its victims' lives, in the slightest changes of habit and behaviour. Invariably there was the same reluctance to go out of doors, the abandonment of job, family and friends, a dislike of daylight, a gradual loss of weight and retreat into a hibernating self. As the illness became more widespread, affecting one in a hundred of the population, blame seemed to lie with the depletion of the ozone layer that had continued apace during the 1980s and 1990s. Perhaps the symptoms of world-shyness and withdrawal were no more than a self-protective response to the hazards of ultraviolet radiation, the psychological equivalent of the sunglasses worn by the blind.

But always there was the exaggerated response to sunlight, the erratic migraines and smarting corneas that hinted at the nervous origins of the malaise. There was the taste for wayward and compulsive hobbies, like the marking of obsessional words in a novel, the construction of pointless arithmetical puzzles on a pocket calculator, the collecting of fragments of TV programmes on a video recorder, and the hours spent playing back particular facial grimaces or shots of staircases.

It was another symptom of the 'space sickness', appearing in its terminal stages, that gave both its popular name and the first real clue to the disease. Almost without exception, the victims became convinced that they had once been astronauts. Thousands of the sufferers lay in their darkened hospital wards, or in the seedy bedrooms of back-street hotels, unaware of the world around them but certain that they had once travelled through space to Mars and Venus, walked beside Armstrong on the Moon. All of them, in their last seconds of consciousness, became calm and serene, and murmured like drowsy passengers at the start of a new voyage, their journey home to the sun.

Sheppard could remember Elaine's final retreat, and his last visit to the white-walled clinic beside the St Lawrence River. They had met only once in the two years since the divorce, and he had not been prepared for the transformation of this attractive and self-possessed dentist into a dreaming adolescent being dressed for her first dance. Elaine smiled brightly at him from her anonymous cot, a white hand trying to draw him on to her pillow.

'Roger, we're going soon. We're leaving together...'

As he walked away through the shadowy wards, listening to the babble of voices, the fragments of half-forgotten space jargon picked up from a hundred television serials, he had felt that the entire human race was beginning its embarkation, preparing to repatriate itself to the sun.

Sheppard recalled his last conversation with the young

director of the clinic, and the weary physician's gesture of irritation, less with Sheppard than with himself and his profession.

'A *radical* approach? I assume you're thinking of something like resurrection?' Seeing the suspicious tic that jumped across Sheppard's cheek, Martinsen had taken him by the arm in a show of sympathy. 'I'm sorry – she was a remarkable woman. We talked for many hours, about you, much of the time ...' His small face, as intense as an undernourished child's, was broken by a bleak smile.

Before Sheppard left the clinic the young physician showed him the photographs he had taken of Elaine sitting in a deckchair on the staff lawn earlier that summer. The first hint of radiant good humour was already on her vivid lips, as if this saucy dentist had been quietly tasting her own laughing gas. Martinsen had clearly been most impressed by her.

But was he on the wrong track, like the whole of the medical profession? The ECT treatments and sensory deprivation, the partial lobotomies and hallucinatory drugs all seemed to miss the point. It was always best to take the mad on their own terms. What Elaine and the other victims were trying to do was to explore space, using their illness as an extreme metaphor with which to construct a space vehicle. The astronaut obsession was the key. It was curious how close the whole malaise was to the withdrawal symptoms shown by the original astronauts in the decades after the Apollo programme, the retreat into mysticism and silence. Could it be that travelling into outer space, even thinking about and watching it on television, was a forced evolutionary step with unforeseen consequences, the eating of a very special kind of forbidden fruit? Perhaps, for the central nervous system, space was not a linear structure at all, but a model for an advanced condition of time, a metaphor for eternity which they were wrong to try to grasp...

Looking back, Sheppard realized that for years he had been waiting for the first symptoms of the malaise to affect him, that he was all too eager to be inducted into the great voyage towards the sun. During the months before the divorce he had carefully observed the characteristic signs – the loss of weight and appetite, his cavalier neglect of both staff and clients at his architect's practice, his growing reluctance to go out of doors, the allergic skin rashes that sprang up if he stood for even a few seconds in the open sunlight. He tagged along on Elaine's expeditions to Algonquin Park, and spent the entire weekends sealed inside the chromium womb of the Airstream, itself so like an astronaut's capsule.

Was Elaine trying to provoke him? She hated his forced absentmindedness, his endless playing with bizarre clocks and architectural follies, and above all his interest in pornography. This sinister hobby had sprung out of his peculiar obsession with the surrealists, a school of painters which his entire education and cast of mind had previously closed to him. For some reason he found himself gazing for hours at reproductions of Chirico's Turin, with its empty colonnades and reversed perspectives, its omens of departure. Then there were Magritte's dislocations of time and space, his skies transformed into a series of rectilinear blocks, and Dali's biomorphic anatomies.

These last had led him to his obsession with pornography. Sitting in the darkened bedroom, blinds drawn against the festering sunlight that clung to the balconies of the condominium, he gazed all day at the video-recordings of Elaine at her dressing-table and in the bathroom. Endlessly he played back the zooms and close-ups of her squatting on the bidet, drying herself on the edge of the bath, examining with a hopeful frown the geometry of her right breast. The magnified images of this huge hemisphere, its curvatures splayed between Sheppard's fingers, glowed against the walls and ceiling of the bedroom.

Eventually, even the tolerant Elaine had rebelled. 'Roger, what are you doing to yourself – and to me? You've turned

15

this bedroom into a porno-cinema, with me as your star.' She held his face, compressing twenty years of affection into her desperate hands. 'For God's sake, see someone!'

But Sheppard already had. In the event, three months later, it was Elaine who had gone. At about the time that he closed his office and summarily sacked his exhausted staff, she packed her bags and stepped away into the doubtful safety of the bright sunlight.

Soon after, the space trauma recruited another passenger. Sheppard had last seen her at Martinsen's clinic, but within only six months he received news of her remarkable recovery, no doubt one of those temporary remissions that sometimes freed the terminal cases from their hospital beds. Martinsen had abandoned his post at the clinic, against the open criticism of his colleagues and allegations of misconduct. He and Elaine had left Canada and moved south to the warm Florida winter, and were now living near the old Space Centre at Cape Kennedy. She was up and about, having miraculously shaken off the deep fugues.

At first Sheppard was sceptical, and guessed that the young neurosurgeon had become obsessed with Elaine and was trying some dangerous and radical treatment in a misguided attempt to save her. He imagined Martinsen abducting Elaine, lifting the drowsy but still beautiful woman from her hospital bed and carrying her out to his car, setting off for the harsh Florida light.

However, Elaine seemed well enough. During this period of apparent recovery she wrote several letters to Sheppard, describing the dark, jewelled beauty of the overgrown forest that surrounded their empty hotel, with its view over the Banana River and the rusting gantries of the abandoned Space Centre. Reading her final letter in the flinty light of the Toronto spring, it seemed to Sheppard that the whole of Florida was transforming itself for Elaine into a vast replica of the cavernous grottoes of Gustave Moreau, a realm of opalized palaces and heraldic animals.

'...I wish you could be here, Roger, this forest is filled with a deep marine light, almost as if the dark lagoons that once covered the Florida peninsula have come in from the past and submerged us again. There are strange creatures here that seem to have stepped off the surface of the sun. Looking out over the river this morning, I actually saw a unicorn walking on the water, its hooves shod in gold. Philip has moved my bed to the window, and I sit propped here all day, courting the birds, species I've never seen before that seem to have come from some extraordinary future. I feel sure now that I shall never leave here. Crossing the garden yesterday, I found that I was dressed in light, a sheath of golden scales that fell from my skin on to the glowing grass. The intense sunlight plays strange tricks with time and space. I'm really certain that there's a new kind of time here, flowing in some way from the old Space Centre. Every leaf and flower, even the pen in my hand and these lines I'm writing to you are surrounded by haloes of themselves.

Everything moves very slowly now, it seems to take all day for a bird to cross the sky, it begins as a shabby little sparrow and transforms itself into an extravagant creature as plumed and ribboned as a lyre-bird. I'm glad we came, even though Philip was attacked at the time. Coming here was my last chance, he claims, I remember him saying we should seize the light, not fear it. All the same, I think he's got more than he bargained for, he's very tired, poor boy. He's frightened of my falling asleep, he says that when I dream I try to turn into a bird. I woke up by the window this afternoon and he was holding me down, as if I were about to fly off for ever into the forest.

I wish you were here, dear, it's a world the surrealists might have invented. I keep thinking that I will meet you somewhere...

Attached to the letter was a note from Martinsen, telling

him that Elaine had died the following day, and that at her request she had been buried in the forest near the Space Centre. The death certificate was counter-signed by the Canadian consul in Miami.

A week later Sheppard closed the Toronto apartment and set off for Cape Kennedy. During the past year he had waited impatiently for the malaise to affect him, ready to make his challenge. Like everyone else he rarely went out during the day, but through the window blinds the sight of this empty, sunlit city which came alive only at dusk drove Sheppard into all kinds of restless activity. He would go out into the noon glare and wander among the deserted office blocks, striking stylized poses in the silent curtain-walling. A few heavily cowled policemen and taxi-drivers watched him like spectres on a furnace floor. But Sheppard liked to play with his own obsessions. On impulse he would run around the apartment and release the blinds, turning the rooms into a series of white cubes, so many machines for creating a new kind of time and space.

Thinking of all that Elaine had said in her last letter, and determined as yet not to grieve for her, he set off eagerly on his journey south. Too excited to drive himself, and wary of the steeper sunlight, he moved by bus, rented limousine and taxi. Elaine had always been an accurate observer, and he was convinced that once he reached Florida he would soon rescue her from Martinsen and find respite for them both in the eternal quiet of the emerald forest.

In fact, he found only a shabby, derelict world of dust, drained swimming-pools and silence. With the end of the Space Age thirty years earlier, the coastal towns near Cape Kennedy had been abandoned to the encroaching forest. Titusville, Cocoa Beach and the old launching grounds now constituted a psychic disaster area, a zone of ill omen. Lines of deserted bars and motels sat in the heat, their signs like rusty toys. Beside the handsome houses once owned by flight controllers and astrophysicists the empty swimming-

18

pools were a resting-place for dead insects and cracked sunglasses.

Shielded by the coat over his head, Sheppard paid off the uneasy cab driver. As he fumbled with his wallet the un-latched suitcase burst at his feet, exposing its contents to the driver's quizzical gaze: a framed reproduction of Magritte's *The March of Summer*, a portable video-cassette projector, two tins of soup, a well-thumbed set of six *Kamera Klassic* magazines, a clutch of cassettes labelled *Elaine/Shower Stall I–XXV*, and a paperback selection of Marey's *Chronograms*.

The driver nodded pensively. 'Samples? Exactly what is all that — a survival kit?'

'Of a special kind.' Unaware of any irony in the man's voice, Sheppard explained: 'They're the fusing device for a time-machine. I'll make one up for you ...'

'Too late. My son ...' With a half-smile, the driver wound up his tinted windows and set off for Tampa in a cloud of glassy dust.

Picking the Starlight Motel at random, Sheppard let himself into an intact cabin overlooking the drained pool, the only guest apart from the elderly retriever that dozed on the office steps. He sealed the blinds and spent the next two days resting in the darkness on the musty bed, the suitcase beside him, this 'survival kit' that would help him to find Elaine.

At dusk on the second day he left the bed and went to the window for his first careful look at Cocoa Beach. Through the plastic blinds he watched the shadows bisecting the empty pool, drawing a broken diagonal across the canted floor. He remembered his few words to the cab driver. The complex geometry of this three-dimensional sundial seemed to contain the operating codes of a primitive time-machine, repeated a hundred times in all the drained swimming pools of Cape Kennedy.

Surrounding the motel was the shabby coastal town, its

derelict bars and stores shielded from the sub-tropical dusk by the flamingo-tinted parasols of the palm trees that sprang through the cracked roads and sidewalks. Beyond Cocoa Beach was the Space Centre, its rusting gantries like old wounds in the sky. Staring at them through the sandy glass, Sheppard was aware for the first time of the curious delusion that he had once been an astronaut, lying on his contour couch atop the huge booster, dressed in a suit of silver foil...An absurd idea, but the memory had come from somewhere. For all its fearfulness, the Space Centre was a magnetic zone.

But where was the visionary world which Elaine had described, filled with jewelled birds? The old golden retriever sleeping under the diving board would never walk the Banana River on golden hooves.

Although he rarely left the cabin during the day – the Florida sunlight was still far too strong for him to attempt a head-on confrontation – Sheppard forced himself to put together the elements of an organized life. First, he began to take more care of his own body. His weight had been falling for years, part of a long decline that he had never tried to reverse. Standing in front of the bathroom mirror, he stared at his unsavoury reflection – his wasted shoulders, sallow arms and inert hands, but a fanatic's face, unshaven skin stretched across the bony points of his jaw and cheeks, orbits like the entrances to forgotten tunnels from which gleamed two penetrating lights. Everyone carried an image of himself that was ten years out of date, but Sheppard felt that he was growing older and younger at the same time – his past and future selves had arranged a mysterious rendezvous in this motel bedroom.

Still, he forced down the cold soup. He needed to be strong enough to drive a car, map the forests and runways of Cape Kennedy, perhaps hire a light aircraft and carry out an aerial survey of the Space Centre.

At dusk, when the sky seemed to tilt and, thankfully,

20

tipped its freight of cyclamen clouds into the Gulf of Mexico, Sheppard left the motel and foraged for food in the abandoned stores and supermarkets of Cocoa Beach. A few of the older townspeople lived on in the overgrown side-streets, and one bar was still open to the infrequent visitors. Derelicts slept in the rusting cars, and the occasional tramp wandered like a schizophrenic Crusoe among the wild palms and tamarinds. Long-retired engineers from the Space Centre, they hovered in their shabby whites by the deserted stores, forever hesitating to cross the shadowy streets.

As he carried a battery charger from an untended appliance store, Sheppard almost bumped into a former mission controller who had frequently appeared on television during the campaign to prevent the disbandment of NASA. With his dulled face, eyes crossed by the memories of forgotten trajectories, he resembled one of Chirico's mannequins, heads marked with mathematical formulae.

'No...' He wavered away, and grimaced at Sheppard, the wild fracture lines in his face forming the algebra of an unrealizable future. 'Another time... seventeen seconds...' He tottered off into the dusk, tapping the palm trees with one hand, preoccupied with this private countdown.

For the most part they kept to themselves, twilight guests of the abandoned motels where no rent would ever be charged and no memories ever be repaid. All of them avoided the government aid centre by the bus depot. This unit, staffed by a psychologist from Miami University and two graduate students, distributed food parcels and medicines to the aged townspeople asleep on their rotting porches. It was also their task to round up the itinerant derelicts and persuade them to enter the state-run hospice in Tampa.

On his third evening, as he looted the local supermarket, Sheppard became aware of this alert young psychologist watching him over the dusty windshield of her jeep.

21

'Do you need any help breaking the law?' She came over and peered into Sheppard's carton. 'I'm Anne Godwin, hello. Avocado purée, rice pudding, anchovies, you're all set for a midnight feast. But what about a filet steak, you really look as if you could use one?'

Sheppard tried to sidestep out of her way. 'Nothing to worry about. I'm here on a working vacation ... a scientific project.'

She eyed him shrewdly. 'Just another summer visitor – though you all have PhDs, the remittance men of the Space Age. Where are you staying? We'll drive you back.'

As Sheppard struggled with the heavy carton she signalled to the graduate students, who strolled across the shadowy pavement. At that moment a rusty Chevrolet turned into the street, a bearded man in a soft hat at the wheel. Blocked by the jeep, he stopped to reverse the heavy sedan, and Sheppard recognized the young physician he had last seen on the steps of the clinic overlooking the St Lawrence.

'Dr Martinsen!' Anne Godwin shouted as she released Sheppard's arm. 'I've been wanting to talk to you, doctor. Wait ... ! That prescription you gave me, I take it you've reached the menopause –'

Punching the locked gear shift, Martinsen seemed only interested in avoiding Anne Godwin and her questions. Then he saw Sheppard's alert eyes staring at him above the carton. He paused, and gazed back at Sheppard, with the frank and almost impatient expression of an old friend who had long since come to terms with some act of treachery. He had grown his beard, as if to hide some disease of the mouth or jaw, but his face seemed almost adolescent and at the same time aged by some strange fever.

'Doctor ... I've reported –' Anne Godwin reached Martinsen's car. He made a half-hearted attempt to hide a loosely tied bundle of brass curtain-rods on the seat beside him. Was he planning to hang the forest with priceless fabrics? Before Sheppard could ask, Martinsen engaged his gear lever and sped off, clipping Anne Godwin's out-stretched hand with his wing-mirror.

But at least he knew now that Martinsen was here, and their brief meeting allowed Sheppard to slip away unob-served from Anne Godwin. Followed by the doddery re-triever, Sheppard carried his stores back to the motel, and the two of them enjoyed a tasty snack in the darkness beside the drained swimming-pool.

Already he felt stronger, confident that he would soon have tracked down Martinsen and rescued Elaine. For the next week he slept during the mornings and spent the after-noons repairing the old Plymouth he had commandeered from a local garage.

As he guessed, Martinsen soon put in another appear-ance. A small, bird-shaped kite began a series of regular flights in the sky above Cocoa Beach. Its silver line disap-peared into the forest somewhere to the north of the town. Two others followed it into the air, and the trio swayed across the placid sky, flown by some enthusiast in the forest.

In the days that followed, other bird-emblems began to appear in the streets of Cocoa Beach, crude Picasso doves chalked on the boarded store-fronts, on the dusty roofs of the cars, in the leafy slime on the drained floor of the Starlight pool, all of them presumably cryptic messages from Martinsen.

So the neurosurgeon was trying to lure him into the forest? Finally giving in to his curiosity, Sheppard drove late one afternoon to the light airfield at Titusville. Little traffic visited the shabby airstrip, and a retired commercial pilot dozed in his dusty office below a sign advertising pleasure trips around the Cape.

After a brief haggle, Sheppard rented a single-engined Cessna and took off into the softening dusk. He carried out a careful reconnaissance of the old Space Centre, and at last saw the strange nightclub in the forest, and caught a painful

23

glimpse of the weird, bald-headed spectre racing through the trees. Then Martinsen sprang his surprise with the man-powered glider, clearly intending to ambush Sheppard and force him to crash-land the Cessna into the jungle. However, Sheppard escaped, and limped back to Cocoa Beach and the incoming tide. Anne Godwin virtually dragged him from the swamped plane, but he managed to pacify her and slip away to the motel.

That evening he rested in his chair beside the empty pool, watching the video-cassettes of his wife projected on to the wall at the deep end. Somewhere in these intimate conjunctions of flesh and geometry, of memory, tenderness and desire, was a key to the vivid air, to that new time and space which the first astronauts had unwittingly revealed here at Cape Kennedy, and which he himself had glimpsed that evening from the cockpit of the drowned aircraft.

At dawn Sheppard fell asleep, only to be woken two hours later by a sudden shift of light in the darkened bedroom. A miniature eclipse of the sun was taking place. The light flickered, trembling against the window. Lying on the bed, Sheppard saw the profile of a woman's face and plumed hair projected on to the plastic blinds.

Bracing himself against the eager morning sunlight, and any unpleasant phobic rush, Sheppard eased the blinds apart. Two hundred feet away, suspended above the chairs on the far side of the swimming pool, a large man-carrying kite hung in the air. The painted figure of a winged woman was silhouetted against the sun's disc, arms outstretched across the canvas panels. Her shadow tapped the plastic blinds, only inches from Sheppard's fingers, as if asking to be let into the safety of the darkened bedroom.

Was Martinsen offering him a lift in this giant kite? Eyes shielded behind his heaviest sunglasses, Sheppard left the cabin and made his way around the drained pool. It was

24

time now to make a modest challenge to the sun. The kite hung above him, flapping faintly, its silver wire disappearing behind a boat-house half a mile along the beach.

Confident of himself, Sheppard set off along the beach road. During the night the Cessna had vanished, swept away by the sea. Behind the boat-house the kite-flier was winding in his huge craft, and the woman's shadow kept Sheppard company, the feathered train of her hair at his feet. Already he was sure that he would find Martinsen among the derelict speedboats, ravelling in whatever ambiguous message he had sent up into the fierce air.

Almost tripping over the woman's shadow, Sheppard paused to gaze around him. After so many weeks and months of avoiding the daylight, he felt uncertain of the overlit perspectives, of the sea lapping at the edges of his mind, its tongues flicking across the beach like some treacherous animal's. Ignoring it, he ran along the road. The kite-flier had vanished, slipping away into the palm-filled streets.

Sheppard threw away his sunglasses and looked up into the air. He was surprised that the sky was far closer to him than he remembered. It seemed almost vertical, constructed of cubicular blocks a mile in width, the wall of an immense inverted pyramid.

The waves pressed themselves into the wet sand at his feet, flattering courtiers in this palace of light. The beach seemed to tilt, the road reversed its camber. He stopped to steady himself against the roof of an abandoned car. His retinas smarted, stung by thousands of needles. A feverish glitter rose from the roofs of the bars and motels, from the rusty neon signs and the flinty dust at his feet, as if the whole landscape was at the point of ignition.

The boat-house swayed towards him, its roof tilting from side to side. Its cavernous doors opened abruptly, like the walls of an empty mountain. Sheppard stepped back, for a moment blinded by the darkness, as the figure of a winged man burst from the shadows and raced past him across the

25

sand towards the safety of the nearby forest. Sheppard saw a bearded face under the feathered head-dress, canvas wings on a wooden frame attached to the man's arms. Waving them up and down like an eccentric aviator, he sprinted between the trees, hindered more than helped by his clumsy wings, one of which sheared from his shoulder when he trapped himself among the palms. He vanished into the forest, still leaping up and down in an attempt to gain the air with his one wing.

Too surprised to laugh at Martinsen, Sheppard ran after him. He followed the line of metal thread that unravelled behind the neurosurgeon. The man-carrying kite had collapsed across the roof of a nearby drugstore, but Sheppard ignored it and ran on through the narrow streets. The line came to an end under the rear wheel of an abandoned truck, but he had already lost Martinsen.

On all sides were the bird-signs, chalked up on the fences and tree-trunks, hundreds of them forming a threatening aviary, as if Martinsen was trying to intimidate the original tenants of the forest and drive them away from the Cape. Sheppard sat on the running-board of the truck, holding the broken end of the kite-line between his fingers.

Why was Martinsen wearing his ludicrous wings, trying to turn himself into a bird? At the end of the road he had even constructed a crude bird-trap, large enough to take a condor, or a small winged man, a cage the size of a garden shed tilted back on a trip-balance of bamboo sticks.

Shielding his eyes from the glare, Sheppard climbed on to the bonnet of the truck and took his bearings. He had entered an unfamiliar part of Cocoa Beach, a maze of roads invaded by the forest. He was well within that zone of vibrant light he had seen from the Cessna, the dim lantern that seemed to extend outwards from the Space Centre, illuminating everything it touched. The light was deeper but more resonant, as if every leaf and flower were a window into a furnace.

Facing him, along the line of shabby bars and stores, was a curious laundromat. Sandwiched between a boarded-up appliance store and a derelict cafeteria, it resembled a miniature temple, with a roof of gilded tiles, chromium doors and windows of finely etched glass. The whole structure was suffused with a deep interior light, like some lamp-lit grotto in a street of shrines.

The same bizarre architecture was repeated in the nearby roads that lost themselves in the forest. A dry-goods store, a filling station and a car-wash glittered in the sunlight, apparently designed for some group of visiting space enthusiasts from Bangkok or Las Vegas. Overgrown by the tamarinds and Spanish moss, the gilded turrets and metalled windows formed a jewelled suburb in the forest.

Giving up his search for Martinsen, who by now could be hiding atop one of the Apollo gantries, Sheppard decided to return to his motel. He felt exhausted, as if his body were swathed in a heavy armour. He entered the pavilion beside the cafeteria, smiling at the extravagant interior of this modest laundromat. The washing-machines sat within bowers of ironwork and gilded glass, a series of side-chapels set aside for the worship of the space engineers' overalls and denims.

A ruby light glimmered around Sheppard, as if the pavilion were vibrating above a mild ground-quake. Sheppard touched the glassy wall with one hand, surprised to find that his palm seemed to merge with the surface, as if both were images being projected on to a screen. His fingers trembled, a hundred outlines superimposed upon one another. His feet drummed against the floor, sending the same rapid eddies through his legs and hips, as if he were being transformed into a holographic image, an infinity of replicas of himself. In the mirror above the cashier's metal desk, now a Byzantine throne, he glowed like an archangel. He picked up a glass paperweight from the desk, a tremulous jewel of vibrating coral that suddenly flushed within its own red sea.

The ruby light that radiated from every surface within the laundromat was charged by his own bloodstream as it merged into the flicker of multiplying images.

Staring at his translucent hands, Sheppard left the pavilion and set off along the street through the intense sunlight. Beyond the tilting fences he could see the drained swimming-pools of Cocoa Beach, each a complex geometry of light and shadow, canted decks encoding the secret entrances to another dimension. He had entered a city of yantras, cosmic dials sunk into the earth outside each house and motel for the benefit of devout time-travellers.

The streets were deserted, but behind him he heard a familiar laboured pad. The old retriever plodded along the sidewalk, its coat shedding a tremulous golden fur. Sheppard stared at it, for a moment certain that he was seeing the unicorn Elaine had described in her last letter. He looked down at his wrists, at his incandescent fingers. The sun was annealing plates of copper light to his skin, dressing his arms and shoulders in a coronation armour. Time was condensing around him, a thousand replicas of himself from the past and future had invaded the present and clasped themselves to him.

Wings of light hung from his shoulders, feathered into a golden plumage drawn from the sun, the reborn ghosts of his once and future selves, conscripted to join him here in the streets of Cocoa Beach.

Startled by Sheppard, an old woman stared at him from the door of a shack beside the boat-house. Brittle hands felt her blue-rinsed hair, she found herself transformed from a shabby crone into a powdered beauty from the forgotten Versailles of her youth, her thousand younger selves from every day of her life gladly recruited to her side, flushing her withered cheeks and warming her stick-like hands. Her elderly husband gazed at her from his rocker chair, recognizing her for the first time in decades, himself transformed into a conquistador half-asleep beside a magical sea.

Sheppard waved to them, and to the tramps and derelicts emerging into the sunlight from their cabins and motel rooms, drowsy angels each awaking to his own youth. The flow of light through the air had begun to slow, layers of time overlaid each other, laminae of past and future fused together. Soon the tide of photons would be still, space and time would set forever.

Eager to become part of this magnetic world, Sheppard raised his wings and turned to face the sun.

'Were you trying to fly?'

Sheppard sat against the wall beside his bed, arms held tight like crippled wings around his knees. Near by in the darkened bedroom were the familiar pieces of furniture, the Marey and Magritte reproductions pinned to the dressing-table mirror, the projector ready to screen its black coil of film on to the wall above his head.

Yet the room seemed strange, a cabin allocated to him aboard a mysterious liner, with this concerned young psychologist sitting at the foot of the bed. He remembered her jeep in the dusty road, the loudhailer blaring at the elderly couple and the other derelicts as they were all about to rise into the air, a flight of angels. Suddenly a humdrum world had returned, his past and future selves had fled from him, he found himself standing in a street of shabby bars and shacks, a scarecrow with an old dog. Stunned, the tramps and the old couple had pinched their dry cheeks and faded back to their dark bedrooms.

So this was present time. Without realizing it, he had spent all his life in this grey, teased-out zone. However, he stilll held the paperweight in his hand. Though inert now, raised to the light it began to glow again, summoning its brief past and limitless future to its own side.

Sheppard smiled at himself, remembering the translucent wings – an illusion, of course, that blur of multiple selves

29

that shimmered from his arms and shoulders, like an immense electric plumage. But perhaps at some time in the future he became a winged man, a glass bird ready to be snared by Martinsen? He saw himself caged in the condortraps, dreaming of the sun...

Anne Godwin was shaking her head to herself. She had turned from Sheppard and was examining with evident distaste the pornographic photographs pinned to the wardrobe doors. The glossy prints were overlaid by geometric diagrams which this strange tenant of the motel had pencilled across the copulating women, a secondary anatomy.

'So this is your laboratory? We've been watching you for days. Who are you, anyway?'

Sheppard looked up from his wrists, remembering the golden fluid that had coursed through the now sombre veins.

'Roger Sheppard.' On an impulse he added: 'I'm an astronaut.'

'Really?' Like a concerned nurse, she sat on the edge of the bed, tempted to touch Sheppard's forehead. 'It's surprising how many of you come to Cape Kennedy – bearing in mind that the space programme ended thirty years ago.'

'It hasn't ended.' Quietly, Sheppard did his best to correct this attractive but confused young woman. He wanted her to leave, but already he saw that she might be useful. Besides, he was keen to help her, and set her free from this grey world. 'In fact, there are thousands of people involved in a new programme – we're at the beginnings of the first true Space Age.'

'Not the second? So the Apollo flights were...?'

'Misconceived.' Sheppard gestured at the Marey chronograms on the dressing-table mirror, the blurred time-lapse photos so like the images he had seen of himself before Anne Godwin's arrival. 'Space exploration is a branch of applied geometry, with many affinities to pornography.'

'That sounds sinister.' She gave a small shudder. 'These

photographs of yours look like the recipe for a special kind of madness. You shouldn't go out during the day. Sunlight inflames the eyes – and the mind.'

Sheppard pressed his face against the cool wall, wondering how to get rid of this over-concerned young psychologist. His eyes ran along the sills of light between the plastic blinds. He no longer feared the sun, and was eager to get away from this dark room. His real self belonged to the bright world outside. Sitting here, he felt like a static image in a single frame hanging from the coil of film in the projector on the bedside table. There was a sense of stop-frame about the whole of his past life – his childhood and schooldays, McGill and Cambridge, the junior partnership in Vancouver, his courtship of Elaine, together seemed like so many clips run at the wrong speed. The dreams and ambitions of everyday life, the small hopes and failures, were attempts to bring these separated elements into a single whole again. Emotions were the stress lines in this overstretched web of events.

'Are you all right? Poor man, can't you breathe?'

Sheppard became aware of Anne Godwin's hand on his shoulder. He had clenched his fingers so tightly around the paperweight that his fist was white. He relaxed his grip and showed her the glassy flower.

Casually, he said: 'There's some curious architecture here – filling stations and laundromats like Siamese temples. Have you seen them?'

She avoided his gaze. 'Yes, to the north of Cocoa Beach. But I keep away from there.' She added reluctantly: 'There's a strange light by the Space Centre, one doesn't know whether to believe one's eyes.' She weighed the flower in her small hand, the fingers still bruised by Martinsen's wing-mirror. 'That's where you found this? It's like a fossil of the future.'

'It is.' Sheppard reached out and took it back. He needed the security of the piece, it reminded him of the luminous world from which this young woman had disturbed him. Perhaps she would join him there? He looked up at her strong forehead and high-bridged nose, a cut-prow that could outstare the time-winds, and at her broad shoulders, strong enough to bear a gilded plumage. He felt a sudden urge to examine her, star her in a new video film, explore the planes of her body like a pilot touching the ailerons and fuselage of an unfamiliar aircraft.

He stood up and stepped to the wardrobe. Without thinking, he began to compare the naked figure of his wife with the anatomy of the young woman sitting on his bed, the contours of her breasts and thighs, the triangles of her neck and pubis.

'Look, do you mind?' She stood between Sheppard and the photographs. 'I'm not going to be annexed into this experiment of yours. Anyway, the police are coming to search for that aircraft. Now, what is all this?'

'I'm sorry.' Sheppard caught himself. Modestly, he pointed to the elements of his 'kit', the film strips, chronograms and pornographic photos, the Magritte reproduction. 'It's a machine, of a kind. A time-machine. It's powered by that empty swimming-pool outside. I'm trying to construct a metaphor to bring my wife back to life.'

'Your wife — when did she die?'

'Three months ago. But she's here, in the forest, somewhere near the Space Centre. That was her doctor you saw the other evening, he's trying to turn into a bird.' Before Anne Godwin could protest Sheppard took her arm and beckoned her to the door of the cabin. 'Come on, I'll show you how the pool works. Don't worry, you'll be outside for only ten minutes — we've all been too frightened of the sun.'

She held his elbow when they reached the edge of the empty pool, her face beginning to fret in the harsh light. The floor of the pool was strewn with leaves and discarded sunglasses, in which the diagram of a bird was clearly visible.

Sheppard breathed freely in the gold-lit air. There were no kites in the sky, but to the north of Cocoa Beach he could see the man-powered aircraft circling the forest, its flimsy wings floating on the thermals. He climbed down the chromium ladder into the shallow end of the pool, then helped the nervous young woman after him.

'This is the key to it all,' he explained, as she watched him intently, eyes shielded from the terrifying glare. He felt almost light-headed as he gestured proudly at the angular geometry of white tile and shadow. 'It's an engine, Anne, of a unique type. It's no coincidence that the Space Centre is surrounded by empty swimming-pools.' Aware of a sudden intimacy with this young psychologist, and certain that she would not report him to the police, he decided to take her into his confidence. As they walked down the inclined floor to the deep end he held her shoulders. Below their feet cracked the black lenses of dozens of discarded sunglasses, some of the thousands thrown into the drained swimming-pools of Cocoa Beach like coins into a Roman fountain.

'Anne, there's a door out of this pool, I'm trying to find it, a side-door for all of us to escape through. This space sickness — it's really about time, not space, like all the Apollo flights. We think of it as a kind of madness, but in fact it may be part of a contingency plan laid down millions of years ago, a real space programme, a chance to escape into a world beyond time. Thirty years ago we opened a door in the universe...'

He was sitting on the floor of the drained pool among the broken sunglasses, his back to the high wall of the deep end, talking rapidly to himself as Anne Godwin ran up the sloping floor for the medical valise in her jeep. In his white hands he held the glass paperweight, his blood and the sun charging the flower into a red blaze.

Later, as he rested with her in his bedroom at the motel, and during their days together in the coming week, Sheppard explained to her his attempt to rescue his wife, to find a key to everything going on around them.

'Anne, throw away your watch. Fling back the blinds. Think of the universe as a simultaneous structure. Everything that's ever happened, all the events that *will* ever happen, are taking place together. We can die, and yet still live, at the same time. Our sense of our own identity, the stream of things going on around us, are a kind of optical illusion. Our eyes are too close together. Those strange temples in the forest, the marvellous birds and animals – you've seen them too. We've all got to embrace the sun, I want your children to live here, and Elaine...'

'Roger –' Anne moved his hands from her left breast. For minutes, as he spoke, Sheppard had been obsessively feeling its curvatures, like a thief trying to crack a safe. She stared at the naked body of this obsessive man, the white skin alternating at the elbows and neck with areas of black sunburn, a geometry of light and shade as ambiguous as that of the drained swimming-pool.

'Roger, she died three months ago. You showed me a copy of the death certificate.'

'Yes, she died,' Sheppard agreed. 'But only in a sense. She's here, somewhere, in the total time. No one who has ever lived can ever really die. I'm going to find her, I know she's waiting here for me to bring her back to life...' He gestured modestly to the photographs around the bedroom. 'It may not look much, but this is a metaphor that's going to work.'

During that week, Anne Godwin did her best to help Sheppard construct his 'machine'. All day she submitted to the Polaroid camera, to the films of her body which Sheppard projected on to the wall above the bed, to the endless pornographic positions in which she arranged her thighs and pubis. Sheppard gazed for hours through his stop-frame focus, as if he would find among these images an anatomical door, one of the keys in a combination whose other tumblers were the Marey chronograms, the surrealist paintings and the drained swimming-pool in the ever-brighter sunlight outside. In the evenings Sheppard would take her out into the dusk and pose her beside the empty pool, naked from the waist, a dream-woman in a Delvaux landscape.

Meanwhile, Sheppard's duel with Martinsen continued in the skies above Cape Kennedy. After a storm the drowned Cessna was washed up on to the beach, sections of the wing and tailplane, parts of the cabin and undercarriage. The reappearance of the aircraft drove both men into a frenzy of activity. The bird motifs multiplied around the streets of Cocoa Beach, aerosolled on to the flaking storefronts. The outlines of giant birds covered the beach, their talons gripping the fragments of the Cessna.

And all the while the light continued to grow brighter, radiating outwards from the gantries of the Space Centre, inflaming the trees and flowers and paving the dusty sidewalks with a carpet of diamonds. For Anne, this sinister halo that lay over Cocoa Beach seemed to try to sear itself into her retinas. Nervous of windows, she submitted herself to Sheppard during these last days. It was only when he tried to suffocate her, in a confused attempt to release her past and future selves from their prison, that she escaped from the motel and set off for the sheriff at Titusville.

As the siren of the police car faded through the forest, Sheppard rested against the steering wheel of the Plymouth. He had reached the old NASA causeway across the Banana River, barely in time to turn off on to a disused slip road. He unclenched his fists, uneasily aware that his hands still stung from his struggle with Anne Godwin. If only he had been given more time to warn the young woman that he was trying to help her, to free her from that transient, time-locked flesh he had caressed so affectionately.

Restarting the engine, Sheppard drove along the slip road, already an uneven jungle path. Here on Merrit Island, almost within the sweeping shadows of the great gantries, the forest seemed ablaze with light, a submarine world in which each leaf and branch hung weightlessly around him. Relics of the first Space Age emerged from the undergrowth like overlit ghosts – a spherical fuel tank stitched into a jacket of flowering lianas, rocket launchers collapsed at the feet of derelict gantries, an immense tracked vehicle six storeys high like an iron hotel, whose unwound treads formed two notched metal roads through the forest.

Six hundred yards ahead, when the path petered out below a collapsed palisade of palm trunks, Sheppard switched off the engine and stepped from the car. Now that he was well within the perimeter of the Space Centre he found that the process of time-fusion was even more advanced. The rotting palms lay beside him, but alive again, the rich scrolls of their bark bright with the jade years of youth, glowing with the copper hues of their forest maturity, elegant in the grey marquetry of their declining age.

Through a break in the canopy Sheppard saw the Apollo 12 gantry rising through the high oaks like the blade of a giant sundial. Its shadow lay across a silver inlet of the Banana River. Remembering his flight in the Cessna, Sheppard estimated that the nightclub was little more than a mile to the north-west. He set off on foot through the forest, stepping from one log to the next, avoiding the curtains of Spanish moss that hung out their beguiling frescoes. He crossed a small glade beside a shallow stream, where a large alligator basked contentedly in a glow of self-generated light, smiling to itself as its golden jaws nuzzled its past and future selves. Vivid ferns sprang from the damp humus, ornate leaves stamped from foil, layer upon layer of copper and verdigris annealed together. Even the modest ground-ivy seemed to have glutted itself on the corpses of long-vanished astronauts. This was a world nourished by time.

Bird-signs marked the trees, Picasso doves scrawled on every trunk as if some over-worked removal manager was preparing the entire forest for flight. There were huge traps, set out in the narrow clearings and clearly designed to snare a prey other than birds. Standing by one of the trip-balanced hutches, Sheppard noticed that they all pointed towards the Apollo gantries. So Martinsen was now frightened, not of Sheppard, but of some aerial creature about to emerge from the heart of the Space Centre.

Sheppard tossed a loose branch on to the sensitive balance of the trap. There was a flicker of sprung bamboo, and the heavy hutch fell to the ground in a cloud of leaves, sending a glimmer of light reverberating among the trees. Almost at once there was a flurry of activity from a copse of glowing palmettos a hundred yards away. As Sheppard waited, hidden behind the trap, a running figure approached, a bearded man in a ragged bird costume, half-Crusoe, half-Indian brave, bright macaw feathers tied to his wrists and an aviator's goggles on his forehead.

He raced up to the trap and stared at it in a distraught way. Relieved to find it empty, he brushed the tattered feathers from his eyes and peered at the canopy overhead, as if expecting to see his quarry perched on a nearby branch.

'Elaine...!'

Martinsen's cry was a pathetic moan. Unsure how to calm the neurosurgeon, Sheppard stood up.

'Elaine isn't here, doctor –'

Martinsen flinched back, his bearded face as small as a child's. He stared at Sheppard, barely managing to control himself. His eyes roved across the glowing ground and foliage, and he flicked nervously at the blurred edges of his fingers, clearly terrified of these ghosts of his other selves now clinging to him. He gestured warningly to Sheppard, pointing to the multiple outlines of his arms and legs that formed a glowing armour.

'Sheppard, keep moving. I heard a noise – have you seen Elaine?'

'She's dead, doctor.'

'Even the dead can dream!' Martinsen nodded to Sheppard, his body shaking as if with fever. He pointed to the bird-traps. 'She dreams of flying. I've put these here, to catch her if she tries to escape.'

'Doctor...' Sheppard approached the exhausted physician. 'Let her fly, if she wants to, let her dream. And let her *wake*...'

'Sheppard!' Martinsen stepped back, appalled by Sheppard's electric hand raised towards him. 'She's trying to come back from the dead!'

Before Sheppard could reach him, the neurosurgeon turned away. He smoothed his feathers and darted through the palms, and with a hoot of pain and anger disappeared into the forest.

Sheppard let him go. He knew now why Martinsen had flown his kites, and filled the forest with the images of birds. He had been preparing the whole of the Space Centre for Elaine, transforming the jungle into an aviary where she might be at home. Terrified by the sight of this apparently winged woman waking from her deathbed, he hoped that somehow he could keep her within the magical realm of the Cape Kennedy forest.

Leaving the traps, Sheppard set off through the trees, his eyes fixed on the great gantries now only a few hundred yards away. He could feel the time-winds playing on his skin, annealing his other selves on to his arms and shoulders, the transformation of himself once again into that angelic being who strode through the shabby streets of Cocoa Beach. He crossed a concrete runway and entered an area of deeper forest, an emerald world furnished with extravagant frescoes, a palace without walls.

He had almost ceased to breathe. Here, at the centre of the space grounds, he could feel time rapidly engorging itself. The infinite pasts and future of the forest had fused together. A long-tailed parakeet paused among the branches over his head, an electric emblem of itself more magnificent than a peacock. A jewelled snake hung from a bough, gathering to it all the embroidered skins it had once shed.

An inlet of the Banana River slid through the trees, a silver tongue lying passively at his feet. On the bank fifty yards away was the nightclub he had seen from the Cessna, its luminous façade glowing against the foliage.

Sheppard hesitated by the water's edge, and then stepped on to its hard surface. He felt the brittle corrugations under his feet, as if he were walking across a floor of frosted glass. Without time, nothing could disturb the water. On the quartz-like grass below the nightclub a flock of orioles had begun to rise from the ground. They hung silently in the air, their golden fans lit by the sun.

Sheppard stepped ashore and walked up the slope towards them. A giant butterfly spread its harlequin wings against the air, halted in midflight. Avoiding it, Sheppard strode towards the entrance to the nightclub, where the man-powered glider sat on the grass, its propeller a bright sword. An unfamiliar bird crouched on the canopy, a rare species of quetzal or toucan, only recently a modest starling. It stared at its prey, a small lizard sitting on the steps, now a confident iguana armoured within all its selves. Like everything in the forest, both had become ornamental creatures drained of malice.

Through the crystal doors Sheppard peered into the glowing bower of the nightclub. Already he could see that this exotic pavilion had once been no more than a park-keeper's lodge, some bird-watcher's weekend hide transformed by the light of its gathering identities into this miniature casino. The magic casements revealed a small but opulent chamber, a circle of well-upholstered electric chairs beside a kitchen like the side-chapel of a chromium cathedral. Along the rear

39

wall was a set of disused cages left here years earlier by a local ornithologist.

Sheppard unlatched the doors and stepped into the airless interior. A musty and unpleasant odour hung around him, not the spoor of birds but of some unclaimed carcass stored too long in the sun.

Behind the kitchen, and partly hidden in the shadows thrown by the heavy curtains, was a large cage of polished brass rods. It stood on a narrow platform, with a velvet drape across one end, as if some distracted conjuror had been about to perform an elaborate trick involving his assistant and a flock of doves.

Sheppard crossed the chamber, careful not to touch the glowing chairs. The cage enclosed a narrow hospital cot, its side-panels raised and tightly bolted. Lying on its bare mattress was an elderly woman in a bathrobe. She stared with weak eyes at the bars above her face, hair hidden inside a white towel wrapped securely around her forehead. One arthritic hand had seized the pillow, so that her chin jutted forward like a chisel. Her mouth was open in a dead gape, an ugly rictus that exposed her surprisingly even teeth.

Looking down at the waxy skin of this once familiar face, a part of his life for so many years, Sheppard at first thought that he was looking at the corpse of his mother. But as he pulled back the velvet drape the sunlight touched the porcelain caps of her teeth.

'Elaine ... '

Already he accepted that she was dead, that he had come too late to this makeshift mausoleum where the grieving Martinsen had kept her body, locking it into this cage while he tried to draw Sheppard into the forest.

He reached through the bars and touched her forehead. His nervous hand dislodged the towel, exposing her bald scalp. But before he could replace the grey skull-cloth he felt something seize his wrist. Her right hand, a clutch of knobbly sticks from which all feeling had long expired, moved and took his own. Her weak eyes stared calmly at Sheppard, recognizing this young husband without any surprise. Her blanched lips moved across her teeth, testing the polished cusps, as if she were cautiously identifying herself.

'Elaine...I've come. I'll take you – ' Trying to warm her hand, Sheppard felt an enormous sense of relief, knowing that all the pain and uncertainty of the past months, his search for the secret door, had been worthwhile. He felt a race of affection for his wife, a need to give way to all the stored emotions he had been unable to express since her death. There were a thousand and one things to tell her, about his plans for the future, his uneven health and, above all, his long quest for her across the drained swimming-pools of Cape Kennedy.

He could see the glider outside, the strange bird that guarded the now glowing cockpit, a halo in which they could fly away together. He fumbled with the door to the cage, confused by the almost funereal glimmer that had begun to emanate from Elaine's body. But as she stirred and touched her face, a warm light suffused her grey skin. Her face was softening, the bony points of her forehead re-treated into the smooth temples, her mouth lost its death-grimace and became the bright bow of the young student he had first seen twenty years ago, smiling at him across the tennis club pool. She was a child again, her parched body flushed and irrigated by her previous selves, a lively school-girl animated by the images of her past and future.

She sat up, strong fingers releasing the death-cap around her head, and shook loose the damp tresses of silver hair. She reached her hands towards Sheppard, trying to embrace her husband through the bars. Already her arms and shoulders were sheathed in light, that electric plumage which he now wore himself, winged lover of this winged woman.

As he unlocked the cage, Sheppard saw the pavilion doors open to the sun. Martinsen stood in the entrance, staring at the bright air with the toneless expression of a sleepwalker woken from a dark dream. He had shed his feathers, and his body was now dressed in a dozen glimmering images of himself, refractions of past and present seen through the prism of time.

He gestured to Sheppard, trying to warn him away from his wife. Sheppard was certain now that the physician had been given a glimpse into the dream-time, as he mourned Elaine in the hours after her death. He had seen her come alive from the dead, as the images of her past and youth came to her rescue, drawn here by the unseen powers of the Space Centre. He feared the open cage, and the spectre of this winged woman rising from her dreams at the grave's edge, summoning the legion of her past selves to resurrect her.

Confident that Martinsen would soon understand, Sheppard embraced his wife and lifted her from the bed, eager to let this young woman escape into the sunlight.

Could all this have been waiting for them, around the unseen corners of their past lives? Sheppard stood by the pavilion, looking out at the silent world. An almost tangible amber sea lay over the sandbars of Cape Kennedy and Merrit Island. Hung from the Apollo gantries, a canopy of diamond air stretched across the forest.

There was a glimmer of movement from the river below. A young woman ran along the surface of the water, her silver hair flowing behind her like half-furled wings. Elaine was learning to fly. The light from her outstretched arms glowed on the water and dappled the leaves of the passing trees. She waved to Sheppard, beckoning him to join her, a child who was both his mother and his daughter.

Sheppard walked towards the water. He moved through the flock of orioles suspended above the grass. Each of the stationary birds had become a congested jewel dazzled by its own reflection. He took one of the birds from the air and smoothed its plumage, searching for that same key he had tried to find when he caressed Anne Godwin. He felt the fluttering aviary in his hands, a feathered universe that trembled around a single heart.

The bird shuddered and came to life, like a flower released from its capsules. It sprang from his fingers, a rush of images of itself between the branches. Glad to set it free, Sheppard lifted the orioles down from the air and caressed them one by one. He released the giant butterfly, the quetzal and the iguana, the moths and insects, the frozen, time-locked ferns and palmettos by the water's edge.

Last of all, he released Martinsen. He embraced the helpless doctor, searching for the strong sinews of the young student and the wise bones of the elderly physician. In a sudden moment of recognition, Martinsen found himself, his youth and his age merged in the open geometries of his face, this happy rendezvous of his past and future selves. He stepped back from Sheppard, hands raised in a generous salute, then ran across the grass towards the river, eager to see Elaine.

Content now, Sheppard set off to join them. Soon the forest would be alive again, and they could return to Cocoa Beach, to that motel where Anne Godwin lay in the darkened bedroom. From there they would move on, to the towns and cities of the south, to the sleepwalking children in the parks, to the dreaming mothers and fathers embalmed in their homes, waiting to be woken from the present into the infinite realm of their time-filled selves.

Having a Wonderful Time

3 JULY 1985 Hotel Imperial, Playa Inglaterra, Las Palmas

We arrived an hour ago after an amazing flight. For some reason of its own the Gatwick computer assigned us to first class seats, along with a startled dentist from Bristol, her husband and three children. Richard, as ever fearful of flying, took full advantage of the free champagne and was five miles high before the wheels left the ground. I've marked our balcony on the twenty-seventh floor. It's an extraordinary place, about twenty miles down the coast from Las Palmas, a brand-new resort complex with every entertainment conceivable, all arranged by bedside push-button. I'm just about to dial an hour's water-skiing, followed by Swedish massage and the hairdresser! *Diana*.

10 JULY Hotel Imperial

An unbelievable week! I've never crammed so much excite-ment into a few days — tennis, scuba-diving, water-skiing, rounds of cocktail parties. Every evening a group of us heads for the boîtes and cabarets along the beach, ending up at one or more of the five nightclubs in the hotel. I've hardly seen Richard. The handsome cavalier in the picture is the so-called Beach Counsellor, a highly intelligent ex-public re-lations man who threw it all in two years ago and has been here ever since. This afternoon he's teaching me to hang-glide. Wish me happy landings! *Diana*.

17 JULY Hotel Imperial

The times of sand are running out. Sitting here on the balcony, watching Richard ski-chute across the bay, it's hard to believe we'll be in Exeter tomorrow. Richard swears the first thing he'll do is book next year's holiday. It really has been an amazing success – heaven knows how they do it at the price, there's talk of a Spanish government subsidy. In part it's the unobtrusive but highly sophisticated organization – not a hint of Butlins, though it's British-run and we're all, curiously, from the West Country. Do you realise that Richard and I have been so busy we haven't once bothered to visit Las Palmas? (Late news-flash: Mark Hastings, the Beach Counsellor, has just sent orchids to the room!) I'll tell you all about him tomorrow. *Diana*.

18 JULY Hotel Imperial

Surprise! That computer again. Apparently there's been some muddle at the Gatwick end, our aircraft won't be here until tomorrow at the earliest. Richard is rather worried about not getting to the office today. We blew the last of our traveller's cheques, but luckily the hotel have been marvellous, thanks largely to Mark. Not only will there be no surcharge, but the desk-clerk said they would happily advance us any cash we need. Hey-ho … A slight let-down, all the same. We walked along the beach this afternoon, together for the first time. I hadn't realized how vast this resort complex actually is – it stretches for miles along the coast and half of it's still being built. Everywhere people were coming in on the airport buses from Sheffield and Manchester and Birmingham, within half an hour they're swimming and water-skiing, lounging around the hundreds of pools with their duty-free Camparis. Seeing them from the out-side, as it were, it's all rather strange. *Diana*.

25 JULY Hotel Imperial

Still here. The sky's full of aircraft flying in from Gatwick and Heathrow, but none of them, apparently, is ours. Each morning we've waited in the lobby with our suitcases packed, but the airport bus never arrives. After an hour or so the desk-clerk rings through that there's been a postpone-ment and we trudge back to another day by the pool, drinks and water-skiing on the house. For the first few days it was rather amusing, though Richard was angry and depressed. The company is a major Leyland supplier, and if the axe falls, middle-management is the first to feel it. But the hotel have given us unrestricted credit, and Mark says that as long as we don't go over the top they'll probably never bother to collect. Good news: the company have just cabled Richard telling him not to worry. Apparently hordes of people have been caught the same way. An immense relief — I wanted to phone you, but for days now all the lines have been blocked. *Diana*.

15 AUGUST Hotel Imperial

Three more weeks! Hysterical laughter in paradise…the English papers flown in here are full of it, no doubt you've heard that there's going to be a government inquiry. Appar-ently, instead of flying people back from the Canaries the airlines have been sending their planes on to the Caribbean to pick up the American holiday traffic. So the poor British are stuck here indefinitely. There are literally hundreds of us in the same boat. The amazing thing is that one gets used to it. The hotel people are charm itself, they've pulled out all the stops, organizing extra entertainments of every kind. There's a very political cabaret, and an underwater archae-ology team are going to raise a Spanish caravel from the sea floor. To fill in the time I'm joining an amateur theatrical group, we're thinking of putting on *The Importance of Being Ernest*. Richard takes it all with surprising calm. I wanted to post this from Las Palmas, but there are no buses running, and when we set out on foot Richard and I lost ourselves in a maze of building sites. *Diana*.

5 SEPTEMBER Hotel Imperial

No news yet. Time moves like a dream. Every morning a crowd of bewildered people jam the lobby, trying to find news of their flights back. On the whole, everyone's taking it surprisingly well, showing that true British spirit. Most of them, like Richard, are management people in industry, but the firms, thank heavens, have been absolutely marvellous and cabled us all to get back when we can. Richard comments cynically that with present levels of industrial stagnation, and with the Government footing the bill, they're probably glad to see us here. Frankly, I'm too busy with a hundred and one activities to worry – there's a sort of mini-Renaissance of the arts going on. Mixed saunas, cordon bleu classes, encounter groups, the theatre, of course, and marine biology. Incidentally, we never did manage to get into Las Palmas. Richard hired a pedalo yesterday and set off up the coast. Apparently the entire island is being divided into a series of huge self-contained holiday complexes – human reserves, Richard called them. He estimates that there are a million people here already, mostly English working class from the north and midlands. Some of them have apparently been here for a year, living quite happily, though their facilities are nowhere as good as ours. Dress rehearsal tonight. Think of me as Lady Bracknell – it's mortifying that there's no one else quite mature enough to play the part, they're all in their twenties and thirties, but Tony Johnson, the director, an ex-ICI statistician, is being awfully sweet about it. *Diana*.

6 OCTOBER Hotel Imperial

Just a brief card. There was a crisis this morning when Richard, who's been very moody recently, finally came into collision with the hotel management. When I went into the lobby after my French conversation class a huge crowd had gathered, listening to him rant away at the desk clerks. He was very excited but extremely logical in a mad way, demanding a taxi (there are none here, no one ever goes anywhere) to take him into Las Palmas. Balked, he insisted on being allowed to phone the Governor of the Islands, or the Swiss Consul. Mark and Tony Johnson then arrived with a doctor. There was a nasty struggle for a moment, and then they took him up to our room. I thought he was completely out, but half an hour later, when I left the shower, he'd vanished. I hope he's cooling off somewhere. The hotel management have been awfully good, but it did surprise me that no one tried to intervene. They just watched everything in a glazed way and wandered back to the pool. Sometimes I think they're in no hurry to get home. *Diana.*

12 NOVEMBER Hotel Imperial

An extraordinary thing happened today – I saw Richard for the first time since he left. I was out on the beach for my morning jog when there he was, sitting by himself under an umbrella. He looked very tanned and healthy, but much slimmer. He calmly told me a preposterous story about the entire Canaries being developed by the governments of Western Europe, in collusion with the Spanish authorities, as a kind of permanent holiday camp for their unemployables, not just the factory workers but most of the management people too. According to Richard there is a beach being built for the French on the other side of the island, and another for the Germans. And the Canaries are only one of many sites around the Mediterranean and Caribbean. Once there, the holiday-makers will never be allowed to return home, for fear of starting revolutions. I tried to argue with him, but he casually stood up and said he was going to form a resistance group, then strode away along the beach. The trouble is that he's found nothing with which to occupy his mind – I wish he'd join our theatre group, we're now rehearsing Pinter's *The Birthday Party*. *Diana*.

10 JANUARY 1986 Hotel Imperial

A sad day. I meant to send you a cable, but there's been too much to do. Richard was buried this morning, in the new international cemetery in the hills overlooking the bay. I've marked his place with an X. I'd last seen him two months ago, but I gather he'd been moving around the island, living in the half-constructed hotels and trying unsuccessfully to set up his resistance group. A few days ago he apparently stole an unseaworthy motor-boat and set off for the African coast. His body was washed ashore yesterday on one of the French beaches. Sadly, we'd completely lost touch, though I feel the experience has given me a degree of insight and maturity which I can put to good use when I play Clytemnestra in Tony's new production of *Electra*. He and Mark Hastings have been pillars of strength. *Diana*.

3 JULY 1986 Hotel Imperial

Have I really been here a year? I'm so out of touch with England that I can hardly remember when I last sent a postcard to you. It's been a year of the most wonderful theatre, of parts I would once never have dreamed of playing, and of audiences so loyal that I can hardly bear the thought of leaving them. The hotels are full now, and we play to a packed house every night. There's so much to do here, and everyone is so fulfilled, that I rarely find the time to think of Richard. I very much wish you were here, with Charles and the children – but you probably are, at one of the thousand hotels along the beach. The mails are so erratic, I sometimes think that all my cards to you have never been delivered, but lie unsorted with a million others in the vaults of the shabby post office behind the hotel. Love to all of you. *Diana.*

A Host of Furious Fancies

Don't look now, but an unusual young woman and her elderly companion are sitting down behind us. Every Thursday afternoon they leave the Casino and come here to the café terrace of the Hotel de Paris, always choosing the same two tables near the magazine kiosk. If you lean forward you can see the girl in the restaurant mirror, the tall and elegant one with the too-level gaze and that characteristic walk of rich young women who have been brought up by nuns.

The man is behind her, the seedy-looking fellow with the once-handsome face, at least twenty years older, though you probably think thirty. He wears the same expensive but ill-fitting grey suit and silver tie, as if he has just been let out of some institution to attend a wedding. His eyes follow the secretaries returning from their lunches, plainly dreaming of escape. Observing his sad gaze, one not without a certain dignity, I can only conclude that Monte Carlo is a special kind of prison.

You've seen them now? Then you will agree it's hard to believe that these two are married, and have even achieved a stable union, though of a special kind, and governed by a set of complex rituals. Once a week she drives him from Vence to Monte Carlo in their limousine, that gold-tinted Cadillac parked across the square. After half an hour they emerge from the Casino, when he has played away at the roulette wheels the few francs he has been given. From the kiosk of this café terrace she buys him the same cheap magazine, one

51

of those dreadful concierge rags about servant girls and their Prince Charmings, and then sips at her citron presse as they sit at separate tables. Meanwhile he devours the magazine like a child. Her cool manner is the epitome of a serene self-assurance, of the most robust mental health.

Yet only five years ago, as the physician in charge of her case, I saw her in a very different light. Indeed, it's almost inconceivable that this should be the same young woman whom I first came across at the Hospice of Our Lady of Lourdes, in a state of utter mental degeneration. That I was able to cure her after so many others had failed I put down to an extraordinary piece of psychiatric detection, of a kind that I usually despise. Unhappily, however, that success was bought at a price, paid a hundred times over by the sad old man, barely past his forty-fifth year, who drools over his trashy magazine a few tables behind us.

Before they leave, let me tell you about the case...

By chance, it was only the illness of a colleague that brought me into contact with Christina Brossard. After ten years of practice in Monaco as a successful dermatologist I had taken up a part-time consultancy at the American Clinic in Nice. While looking through the out-patients' roster of an indisposed colleague I was told by his secretary that a 17-year-old patient, one Mlle Brossard, had not arrived for her appointment. At that moment one of the nursing sisters at the Our Lady of Lourdes Hospice at Vence – where the girl had been under care for three years – telephoned to cancel the consultation.

'The Mother Superior asks me to apologize to Prof. Derain but the child is simply too distraught again.'

I thought nothing of it at the time, but for some reason – perhaps the girl's name, or the nun's use of 'again' – I asked for the clinical notes. I noticed that this was the third appointment to be cancelled during the previous year. An orphan, Christina Brossard had been admitted to the Hospice at the age of fourteen after the suicide of her father, who had been her only guardian since the death of her mother in an air-crash.

At this point I remembered the entire tragedy. A former mayor of Lyon, Gaston Brossard was a highly successful building contractor and intimate of President Pompidou's, a millionaire many times over. At the peak of his success this 55-year-old man had married for the third time. For his young bride, a beautiful ex-television actress in her early twenties, he had built a sumptuous mansion above Vence. Sadly, however, only two years after Christina's birth the young mother had died when the company aircraft taking her to join her husband in Paris had crashed in the Alpes Maritimes. Heart-broken, Gaston Brossard then devoted the remaining years of his life to the care of his infant daughter. All had gone well, but twelve years later, for no apparent reason, the old millionaire shot himself in his bedroom.

The effects on the daughter were immediate and disastrous – complete nervous collapse, catatonic withdrawal and a slow but painful recovery in the nearby Hospice of Our Lady of Lourdes, which Gaston Brossard had generously endowed in memory of his young wife. The few clinical notes, jotted down by a junior colleague of Derain's who had conscientiously made the journey to Vence, described a recurrent dermatitis, complicated by chronic anaemia and anorexia.

Sitting in my comfortable office, beyond a waiting-room filled with wealthy middle-aged patients, I found myself thinking of this 17-year-old orphan lost high in the mountains above Nice. Perhaps my anti-clerical upbringing – my father had been a left-wing newspaper cartoonist, my mother a crusading magistrate and early feminist – made me suspicious of the Hospice of Our Lady of Lourdes. The very name suggested a sinister combination of faith-healing and religious charlatanry, almost expressly designed to take advantage of a mentally unbalanced heiress. Lax executors and unconcerned guardians would leave the child ripe for exploitation, while her carefully preserved illness would guarantee the continued flow of whatever funds had been earmarked for the Hospice in Gaston Brossard's will. As I well knew, dermatitis, anorexia and anaemia were all too often convenient descriptions for a lack of hygiene, malnutrition and neglect.

The following weekend, as I set off for Vence in my car – Prof. Derain had suffered a mild heart attack and would be absent for a month – I visualized this wounded child imprisoned above these brilliant hills by illiterate and scheming nuns who had deliberately starved the pining girl while crossing their palms with the dead man's gold dedicated to the memory of the child's mother.

Of course, as I soon discovered, I was totally in error. The Hospice of Our Lady of Lourdes turned out to be a brand new, purpose-built sanatorium with well-lit rooms, sunny grounds and a self-evident air of up-to-date medical practice and devotion to the well-being of the patients, many of whom I could see sitting out on the spacious lawns, talking to their friends and relatives.

The Mother Superior herself, like all her colleagues, was an educated and intelligent woman with a strong, open face and sympathetic manner, and hands – as I always immediately notice – that were not averse to hard work.

'It's good of you to come, Dr Charcot. We've all been worried about Christina for some time. Without any disrespect to our own physicians, it's occurred to me more than once that a different approach may be called for.'

'Presumably, you're referring to chemotherapy,' I suggested. 'Or a course of radiation treatment? One of the few Betatrons in Europe is about to be installed at the Clinic.'

'Not exactly...' The Mother Superior walked pensively

around her desk, as if already reconsidering the usefulness of my visit. 'I was thinking of a less physical approach, Dr Charcot, one concerned to lay the ghosts of the child's spirit as well as those of her body. But you must see her for yourself.'

It was now my turn to be sceptical. Since my earliest days as a medical student I had been hostile to all the claims made by psychotherapy, the happy hunting ground of pseudo-scientific cranks of an especially dangerous kind.

Leaving the Hospice, we drove up into the mountains towards the Brossard mansion, where the young woman was allowed to spend a few hours each day.

'She's extremely active, and tends to unsettle the other patients,' the Mother Superior explained as we turned into the long drive of the mansion, whose Palladian façade presided over a now silent fountain terrace. 'She seems happier here, among the memories of her father and mother.'

We were let into the imposing hall by one of the two young nuns who accompanied the orphaned heiress on these outings. As she and the Mother Superior discussed a patient to be released that afternoon I strolled across the hall and gazed up at the magnificent tapestries that hung from the marbled walls. Above the semi-circular flights of the divided staircase was a huge Venetian clock with ornate hands and numerals like strange weapons, guardians of a fugitive time.

Beyond the shuttered library a colonnaded doorway led to the dining-room. Dustcovers shrouded the chairs and table, and by the fireplace the second of the nuns supervised a servant-girl who was cleaning out the grate. A visiting caretaker or auctioneer had recently lit a small fire of deeds and catalogues. The girl, wearing an old-fashioned leather apron, worked hard on her hands and knees, meticulously sweeping up the cinders before scrubbing the stained tiles.

'Dr Charcot...' The Mother Superior beckoned me into the dining-room. I followed her past the shrouded furniture to the fireplace.

'Sister Julia, I see we're very busy again. Dr Charcot, I'm sure you'll be pleased by the sight of such industry.'

'Of course...' I watched the girl working away, wondering why the Mother Superior should think me interested in the cleaning of a fireplace. The skivvy was little more than a child, but her long, thin arms worked with a will of their own. She had scraped the massive wrought-iron grate with obsessive care, decanting the cinders into a set of transparent plastic bags. Ignoring the three nuns, she dipped a coarse brush into the bucket of soapy water and began to scrub furiously at the tiles, determined to erase the last trace of dirt. The fireplace was already blanched by the soap, as if it had been scrubbed out a dozen times.

I assumed that the child was discharging some penance repeatedly imposed by the Mother Superior. Although not wishing to interfere, I noticed that the girl's hands and wrists showed the characteristic signs of an enzyme-sensitive eczema. In a tone of slight reproof, I remarked: 'You might at least provide a pair of rubber gloves. Now, may I see Mlle Brossard?'

Neither the nuns nor the Mother Superior made any response, but the girl looked up from the soapy tiles. I took in immediately the determined mouth in a pale but once attractive face, the hair fastened fanatically behind a gaunt neck, a toneless facial musculature from which all expression had been deliberately drained. Her eyes stared back at mine with an almost unnerving intensity, as if she had swiftly identified me and was already debating what role I might play for her.

'Christina...' The Mother Superior spoke gently, urging the girl from her knees. 'Dr Charcot has come to help you.'

The girl barely nodded and returned to her scrubbing, pausing only to move the cinder-filled plastic bags out of our reach. I watched her with a professional eye, recalling the diagnosis of dermatitis, anorexia and anaemia. Christina Brossard was thin but not under-nourished, and her pallor was probably caused by all this compulsive activity within the gloomy mansion. As for her dermatitis, this was clearly of that special type caused by obsessive hand-washing.

'Christina – ' Sister Louise, a pleasant, round-cheeked young woman, knelt on the damp tiles. 'My dear, do rest for a moment.'

'No! No! No!' The girl beat the tiles with her soapy brush. She began to wring out the floorcloth, angry hands like bundles of excited sticks. 'There are three more grates to be done this afternoon! You told me to clean them, didn't you, Mother?'

'Yes, dear. It does seem to be what you most want to do.' The Mother Superior stepped back with a defeated smile, giving way to me.

I watched Christina Brossard continue her apparently unending work. She was clearly unbalanced, but somehow self-dramatising at the same time, as if totally gripped by her compulsion but well aware of its manipulative possibilities. I was struck both by her self-pity and by the hard glance which she now and then directed at the three nuns, as if she were deliberately demeaning herself before these pleasant and caring women in order to vent her hate for them.

Giving up for the time being, I left her mopping the tiles and returned to the hall with the Mother Superior.

'Well, Dr Charcot, we're in your hands.'

'I dare say – frankly, I'm not sure that this is a case for me. Tell me – she spends all her time cleaning out these grates?'

'Every day, for the past two years, at her own wish. We've tried to stop her, but she then relapses into her original stupor. We can only assume that it serves some important role for her. There are a dozen fireplaces in this house, each as immaculate as an operating theatre.'

'And the cinders? The bags filled with ash? Who is lighting these fires?'

'Christina herself, of course. She is burning her children's books, determined for some reason to destroy everything she read as a child.'

She led me into the library. Almost the entire stock of books had been removed, and a line of stags' heads gazed down over the empty shelves. One cabinet alone contained a short row of books.

I opened the glass cabinet. There were a few schoolgirl stories, fairy tales, and several childhood classics.

The Mother Superior stared at them sadly. 'There were several hundred originally, but each day Christina burns a few more – under close supervision, it goes without saying, I've no wish to see her burn down the mansion. Be careful not to touch it, but one story alone has remained immune.'

She pointed to a large and shabby illustrated book which had been given a shelf to itself. 'You may see, Dr Charcot, that the choice is not inappropriate – the story of Cinderella.'

As I drove back to Nice, leaving behind that strange mansion with its kindly nuns and obsessed heiress, I found myself revising my opinion of the Mother Superior. This sensible woman was right in believing that all the dermatologists in the world would be unable to free Christina Brossard from her obsession. Clearly the girl had cast herself as Cinderella, reducing herself to the level of the lowest menial. But what guilt was she trying to scrub away? Had she played a still unknown but vital role in the suicide of her father? Was the entire fantasy an unconscious attempt to free herself of her sense of guilt?

I thought of the transparent bags filled with cinders, each one the ashes of a childhood fairy tale. The correspondences were extraordinarily clear, conceived with the remorseless logic of madness. I remembered the hate in her eyes as she stared at the nuns, casting these patient and caring women in the role of the ugly sisters. There was even a wicked stepmother, the Mother Superior, whose Hospice had benefited from the deaths of this orphan's parents.

On the other hand, where were Prince Charming, the fairy godmother and her pumpkin, the ball to be fled from at the stroke of midnight, and above all the glass slipper?

As it happened, I was given no chance to test my hypothesis. Two days later, when I telephoned the Hospice to arrange a new appointment for Christina Brossard, the Mother Superior's secretary politely informed me that the services of the Clinic, of Prof. Derain and myself, would no longer be called upon.

'We're grateful to you, doctor, but the Mother Superior has decided on a new course of treatment. The distinguished psychiatrist Dr Valentina Gabor has agreed to take on the case – perhaps you know of her reputation. In fact, treatment has already begun and you will be happy to hear that Christina is making immediate progress.'

As I replaced the receiver a powerful migraine attacked my left temple. Dr Valentina Gabor – of course I knew of her, the most notorious of the new school of self-styled antipsychiatrists, who devoted whatever time was left over from their endless television appearances to the practice of an utterly bogus psychotherapy, a fashionable blend of post-psychoanalytic jargon, moral uplift and Catholic mysticism. This last strain had presumably gained her the approval of the Mother Superior.

Whenever I saw Dr Valentina my blood began to simmer. This glamorous blonde with her reassuring patter and the eyes of a cashier was forever appearing on television talk shows, putting forward the paradoxical notion that mental illness did not exist but nonetheless was the creation of the patient's family, friends, and even, unbelievably, his doctors. Irritatingly, Dr Valentina had managed to score up a number of authenticated successes, no doubt facilitated by her recent well-publicised audience with the Pope. However, I was confident that she would receive her comeuppance. Already there had been calls within the medical profession for a discreet inquiry into her reported use of LSD and other hallucinogenic drugs.

Nonetheless, it appalled me that someone as deeply ill and as vulnerable as Christina Brossard should fall into the hands of this opportunist quack.

You can well understand, therefore, that I felt a certain satisfaction, not to say self-approval, when I received an urgent telephone call from the Mother Superior some three weeks later.

I had heard no more in the meantime of the Hospice or of Christina. Dr Valentina Gabor, however, had appeared with remorseless frequency on Radio Monte Carlo and the local television channels, spreading her unique brand of psychoanalytic mysticism, and extolling all the virtues of being 'reborn'.

In fact, it was while watching on the late evening news an interview with Dr Gabor recorded that afternoon at Nice Airport before she flew back to Paris that I was telephoned by the Mother Superior.

'Dr Charcot! Thank heavens you're in! There's been a disaster here – Christina Brossard has vanished! We're afraid she may have taken an overdose. I've tried to reach Dr Gabor but she has returned to Paris. Could you possibly come to the Hospice?'

I calmed her as best I could and set off. It was after midnight when I reached the sanatorium. Spotlights filled the drive with a harsh glare, the patients were unsettled, peering through their windows, nuns with torches were fruitlessly searching the grounds. A nervous Sister Louise escorted me to the Mother Superior, who seized my hands with relief. Her strong face was veined with strain.

'Dr Charcot! I'm grateful to you – I only regret that it's so late ...'

'No matter. Tell me what happened. Christina was under Dr Gabor's care?'

'Yes. How I regret my decision. I hoped that Christina might have found herself through a spiritual journey, but I had no idea that drugs were involved. If I had known ...'

She handed me an empty vial. Across the label was Dr Gabor's florid signature.

'We found this in Christina's room an hour ago. She seems to have injected herself with the entire dosage and then driven off wildly into the night. We can only assume that she stole it from Dr Gabor's valise.'

I studied the label. 'Psilocybin – a powerful hallucinogenic drug. Its use is still legal by qualified physicians, though disapproved of by almost the entire profession. This is more than a dangerous toy.'

'Dr Charcot, I know.' The Mother Superior gestured with her worn hands. 'Believe me, I fear for Christina's soul. She appears to have been completely deranged – when she drove off in our oldest laundry van she described it to one of the patients as "her golden carriage".'

'You've called the police?'

'Not yet, Doctor.' A look of embarrassment crossed the Mother Superior's face. 'When Christina left she told one of the orderlies that she was going to "the ball". I'm told that the only ball being held tonight is Prince Rainier's grand gala in Monaco in honour of President Giscard d'Estaing. I assume that she has gone there, perhaps confusing Prince Rainier with the Prince Charming of her fairy tale, and hoping that he will rescue her. It would be profoundly awkward for the Hospice if she were to create a scene, or even try to ...'

'Kill the President? Or the Rainiers? I doubt it.' Already

an idea was forming in my mind. 'However, to be on the safe side I'll leave for Monaco immediately. With luck I'll be there before she can cause any harm to herself.'

Pursued by the Mother Superior's blessings, I returned to my car and set off into the night. Needless to say, I did not intend to make the journey to Monaco. I was quite certain that I knew where Christina Brossard had fled – to her father's mansion above Vence.

As I followed the mountain road I reflected on the evidence that had come together – the fantasy of being a skivvy, the all-promising woman psychiatrist, the hallucinogenic drug. The entire fairy tale of Cinderella was being enacted, perhaps unconsciously, by this deranged heiress. If she herself was Cinderella, Dr Valentina Gabor was the fairy godmother, and her magic wand the hypodermic syringe she waved about so spectacularly. The role of the pumpkin was played by the 'sacred mushroom', the hallucinogenic fungus from which psilocybin was extracted. Under its influence even an ancient laundry van would seem like a golden coach. And as for the 'ball', this of course was the whole psychedelic trip.

But who then was Prince Charming? As I arrived at the great mansion at the end of its drive it occurred to me that I might be unwittingly casting myself in the role, fulfilling a fantasy demanded by this unhappy girl. Holding tight to my medical case, I walked across the dark gravel to the open entrance, where the laundry van had ended its journey in the centre of a flower-bed.

High above, in one of the great rooms facing the sea, a light flickered, as if something was being burned in a grate. I paused in the hall to let my eyes feel their way in the darkness, wondering how best to approach this distraught young woman. Then I saw that the massive Venetian clock above the staircase had been savagely mutilated. Several of the ornate numerals tilted on their mountings. The hands had stopped at midnight, and someone had tried to wrench them from the face.

For all my resistance to that pseudo-science, it occurred to me that once again a psychoanalytic explanation made complete sense of these bizarre events and the fable of Cinderella that underpinned them. I walked up the staircase past the dismembered clock. Despite the fear-crazed assault on them, the erect hands still stood upright on the midnight hour – that time when the ball ended, when the courtships and frivolities of the party were over and the serious business of a real sexual relationship began. Fearful of that male erection, Cinderella always fled at midnight.

But what had Christina Brossard fled from in this Palladian mansion? Suppose that the Prince Charming who courted her so dangerously but so appealingly were in fact her own father. Had some kind of incestuous act involved the widowed industrialist and his adolescent daughter, herself an uncanny image of his dead wife? His revulsion and self-disgust at having committed incest would explain his apparently motiveless suicide *and* his daughter's guilt – as I knew only too well from my court attendances as an expert medical witness, far from hating the fathers who forced them to commit incest, daughters were invariably plagued by powerful feelings of guilt at their responsibility for their parent's imprisonment. So after his death she would naturally return to the house, and try to expiate that guilt as a servant-girl. And what better model for an heiress than Cinderella herself?

Drawn by the distant flames, I crossed the upstairs hallway and entered the great bedroom. It was filled with paintings of young nudes cavorting with centaurs, unmistakably Gaston Brossard's master-bedroom, perhaps where the act of incest had taken place.

Flames lifted from the fireplace, illuminating the ash-streaked face of Christina. She knelt by the grate, crooning

63

as she fed the last of the pages torn from a familiar book of fairy tales. Head to one side, she stared at the soft blaze with overlit eyes, stroking the rough seams of the hospital tunic she wore over her bare legs.

I guessed that she was in the middle of her hallucination and that she saw herself in a resplendent gown. Yet her drifting eyes looked up at me with an expression of almost knowing calm, as if she recognized me and was waiting for me to play my role in the fable and bring it to its proper conclusion. I thought of the mutilated hands of the clock above the staircase. All that remained was to restore the glass slipper to its rightful owner.

Had I now to play the part of her rescuer? Remembering the familiar sexual symbolism of the foot, I knew that the glass slipper was nothing more than a transparent and therefore guilt free vagina. And as for the foot to be placed within it, of course this would not be her own but that of her true lover, the erect male sexual organ from which she fled.

Reaching forward, she added the cover of the fairy tale to the dying blaze, and then looked up at me with waiting eyes. For a moment I hesitated. High on psilocybin, she would be unable to distinguish truth from fantasy, so I could play out my role and bring this psychoanalytic drama to its conclusion without any fear of professional disapproval. My action would not take place in the real world, but within that imaginary realm where the fable of Cinderella was being enacted.

Knowing my role now, and the object which I myself had to place in that glass slipper, I took her hands and drew her from her knees towards her father's bed.

I murmured: 'Cinderella...'

But wait — they're about to leave the terrace. You can look at them now, everyone else is staring frankly at this attractive young woman and her decrepit companion. Sitting here in the centre of Monte Carlo on this magnificent spring day, it's hard to believe that these strange events ever occurred.

It's almost unnerving – she's looking straight at me. But does she recognise me, the dermatologist who freed her from her obsession and restored her to health?

Her companion, sadly, was the only casualty of this radical therapy. As he sits hunched at his table, fumbling with himself like an old man, I can tell you that he was once a fashionable physician whom she met just before her release from the Hospice. They were married three months later, but the marriage was hardly a success. By whatever means, presumably certain methods of her own, she transformed him into this old man.

But why? Simply, that in order to make the incest fantasy credible, any man she marries, however young and princely, however charming, must become old enough to be her father.

Wait! She is coming towards this table. Perhaps she needs my help? She stands in front of the restaurant mirror looking at herself and her elderly husband, and places a hand on his shoulder.

That elegant face with its knowing smile. Let me try to shake that composure, and whisper the title of this cheap magazine on my lap.

'CINDERELLA...'

Her hand pats my shoulder indulgently.

'Father, it's time to go back to the Hospice. I promised the Mother Superior that I wouldn't over-tire you.'

Knowing, elegant, and completely self-possessed.

'And do stop playing that game with yourself. You know it only excites you.'

And very punitive.

Zodiac 2000

Author's note

An updating, however modest, of the signs of the zodiac seems long overdue. The houses of our psychological sky are no longer tenanted by rams, goats and crabs but by helicopters, cruise missiles and intra-uterine coils, and by all the spectres of the psychiatric ward. A few correspondences are obvious – the clones and the hypodermic syringe conveniently take the place of the twins and the archer. But there remains the problem of all those farmyard animals so important to the Chaldeans. Perhaps our true counterparts of these workaday creatures are the machines which guard and shape our lives in so many ways – above all, the taurean computer, seeding its limitless possibilities. As for the ram, that tireless guardian of the domestic flock, his counterpart in our own homes seems to be the Polaroid camera, shepherding our smallest memories and emotions, our most tender sexual acts. Here, anyway, is an s-f zodiac, which I assume the next real one will be…

THE SIGN OF THE POLAROID

The skies were sliding. Already the first of the television crews had arrived in the hospital's car-park and were scanning the upper floors of the psychiatric wing through their binoculars. He lowered the plastic blind, exhausted by all this attention, the sense of a world both narrowing and expanding around him. He waited as Dr Vanessa adjusted the lens of the cine-camera. Her untidy hair, still uncombed since she first collected him from the patients' refectory, fell across the view-finder. Was she placing the filter of her own tissues between herself and whatever threatening message the film might reveal? Since Professor Rotblat's arrival in the Home Office limousine she had done nothing but photograph him obsessively during a range of meaningless activities — studying the tedious Rorschach images, riding the bicycle in the physiology laboratory, squatting across the bidet in her apartment. Why had they suddenly picked him out, an unknown long-term patient whom everyone had ignored since his admission ten years earlier? Throughout his adolescence he had often stood on the roof of the dormitory block and taken the sky into himself, but not even Dr Vanessa had noticed. Pushing back her blonde hair, she looked at him with unexpected concern. 'One last reel, and then you must pack — the helicopter's coming for us.' All night she had sat with him on her bed, projecting the films on to the wall of the apartment.

THE SIGN OF THE COMPUTER

He sat at the metal desk beside the podium, staring at the hushed faces of the delegates as Professor Rotblat gestured with the print-outs. 'A routine cytoplasmic scan was performed six months ago on the patients of this obscure mental institution, as part of the clinical trials of a new antenatal tranquillizer. Thanks to Dr Vanessa Carrington, the extraordinary and wholly anomalous cell chemistry of the subject was brought to my attention, above all the laevorotatory spiral of the DNA helix. The most exhaustive analyses conducted by M.I.T.'s ULTRAC 666, the world's most powerful computer, confirm that this unknown young man, an orphan of untraceable parentage, seems to have been born from a mirror universe, propelled into our own world by cosmic forces of unlimited power. They also indicate that in opting for its original right-hand bias our biological kingdom made the weaker of two choices. All the ULTRAC predictions suggest that the combinative possibilities of laevo-rotatory DNA exceed those of our own cell chemistry by a factor of 10^{27}. I may add that the ULTRAC programmers have constructed a total information model of this alternative universe, with implications that are both exalting and terrifying for us all...'

THE SIGN OF THE CLONES

He steadied himself against the balcony rail, retching on to the turquoise tiles. Twenty feet below his hotel room was the curvilinear roof of the conference centre, its white concrete back like an immense occluded lens. For all Professor Rotblat's talk of alternative universes, the delegates would see nothing through that eye-piece. They seemed to be more impressed by the potency of this over-productive computer than they were by his own. So far his life had been without any possibilities at all — volleyball with the paraplegics, his shins bruised by their wheelchairs, boring hours pretending to paint like Van Gogh in the occupational therapy classes, then evenings spent with TV and largactil. But at least he could look up at the sky and listen to the time-music of the quasars. He waited for the nausea to pass, regretting that he had agreed to be flown here. The lobbies of the hotel were filled with suspiciously deferential officials. Where was Dr Vanessa? Already he missed her reassuring hands, her scent around the projection theatre. He looked up from the vomit on the balcony. Below him the television director was standing on the roof of the conference centre, waving to him in a friendly but cryptic way. There was something uncannily familiar about his face and stance, like a too-perfect reflection in a mirror. At times the man seemed to be mimicking him, trying to signal the codes of an escape combination. Or was he some kind of sinister twin, a right-hand replica of himself being groomed to take his place? Wiping his mouth, he noticed the green pill in the vomit between his feet. So the police orderly had tried to sedate him. Without thinking, he decided to escape, and picked up the manual which the Home Office horoscopist had pushed into his hands after lunch.

THE SIGN OF THE IUD

He could smell her vulva on his hands. He lay on his side in the darkened bedroom, waiting until she returned from the bathroom. Through the glass door he could see her blurred thighs and breasts, as if distorted by some computer permutating all the possibilities of an alternative anatomy. This likeable but strange young woman, with her anonymous apartment and random conversation filled with sudden references to quasars, the overthrow of capitalism, nucleic acids and horoscopy – had she any idea what would soon happen to her? Clearly she had been waiting for him in the hotel's car-park, all too ready to hide him in the jump seat of her sports car. Was she the courier of a rival consortium, sent to him by the unseen powers who presided over the quasars? On the bedside table was the intra-uterine coil, with the draw-string he had felt at the neck of her womb. On some confused impulse she had decided to remove it, as if determined to preserve at least one set of his wild genes within the safekeeping of her placental vault. He swung the coil by its draw-string, this technological cipher that seemed to contain in its double swastika an anagram of all the zodiacal emblems in the horoscopy manual. Was it a clue left for him, a modulus to be multiplied by everything in this right-handed world – the contours of this young woman's breasts, the laws of chemical kinetics, the migration song of swallows? After the camera, the computer and the clones, the coil was the fourth house of that zodiac he had already entered, the twelve-chambered mansion through which he must move with the guile of a master-burglar. He looked up as Renata gently pushed him back on to the pillow. 'Rest for an hour.' She seemed to be forwarding instructions from another sky. 'Then we'll leave for Jodrell Bank.'

THE SIGN OF THE RADAR BOWL

As they waited in the stationary traffic on the crowded deck of the flyover Renata fiddled impatiently with the radio, unable to penetrate the static from the cars around them. Smiling at her, he turned off the sound and pointed to the sky over her head. 'Ignore the horizon. Beyond the Pole Star you can hear the island universes.' He sat back, trying to ignore the thousand satellite transmissions, a barbarous chatter below the great music of the quasars. Even now, through the afternoon sunlight over this provincial city, he could read the comsat relays and the radar beams of Fylingdales and the Norad line in northern Canada, and hear the answering over-the-horizon probes of the Russian sites near Murmansk, distant lions roaring their fear at each other, marking their claims to impossible territories. An incoming missile would be fixed in the cat's cradle of his mind like a fly trapped in the sound-space of a Beethoven symphony. Startled, he saw a pair of scarred hands seize the rim of the windshield. A thick-set man with a hard beard had leapt between the airline buses and was staring at him, his left eye inflamed by some unpleasant virus. To Renata he snapped: 'Get into the back – we've only a week to the First Secretary's visit.'

THE SIGN OF THE STRIPPER

As the music stopped they took their seats in the front row of the strip club. Only three feet from him, on a miniature stage decorated like a boudoir, the naked couple were reaching the climax of their sex act. The bored audience hushed behind them, and he was aware of Heller watching him with an almost obsessive intensity. For days he had been numbed by the galvanic energy of this psychotic man, this terrorist with his doomsday dreams of World War III. During the past few days they had followed a deranged itinerary – airport cargo bays, the approach roads to missile silos, secret apartments packed with computer terminals and guarded by a gang of arrogant killers, hoodlum physicists trained at some deviant university. And above all, the strip clubs – he and Heller had visited dozens of these lurid cabins, watching Renata and the women members of the gang run the gamut of every conceivable sexual variation, perversions so abstract that they had become the elements in a complex calculus. Later, in their apartments, these aggressive women would sidle around him like caricatures from an erotic dream. Already he knew that Heller was trying to recruit him into his conspiracy. But were they unconsciously giving him the keys to the sixth house? He stared up at the young woman who was now leaving the stage to scattered applause, showing off the semen on her thigh. He remembered Heller's frightening violence as he grappled with the young whores in the back of the sports car, assaults as stylized as ballet movements. In the codes of Renata's body, in the junctions of nipple and finger, in the sulcus of her buttocks, waited the possibilities of a benevolent psychopathology.

THE SIGN OF THE PSYCHIATRIST

Professor Rotblat paused as Vanessa Carrington returned from the window and stood behind the young man's chair, her hands protectively on his shoulders. His face seemed to embody the geometry of totally alien obsessions. 'The role of psychiatry today is no longer to cure the patient, but to reconcile him to his strengths and weaknesses, to balance the dark side of the sun against the light – a task, incidentally, made no easier for us by an unaccommodating nature.

Theoretical physics reminds us of the inherent right-hand bias of all matter. The spin of the electron, the rotation of both the solar system and the smallest sub-atomic particles, the great tides that turn the cosmos itself, all embody this fundamental constant, reflected not only in the deep-rooted popular unease with left-handedness, but in the dextro-rotatory helix of DNA. Given the high energies involved, whether in galaxies or biological systems, any attempt at a contrary direction would have catastrophic results, of a type familiar to us in the case of black holes. A single such individual might become the psychological equivalent of a doomsday weapon...' He waited for the young man to reply. Had he returned to the hospital to remind them that he had transcended the role of patient and was moving into a sinistral realm where the ULTRAC predictions should be read from right to left?

THE SIGN OF THE PSYCHOPATH

He stood by the stolen Mercedes as the women loaded the ambassador's body into the trunk. Heller was watching from the elevator doors, the heavy machine-pistol held in both hands. The terrorist's swarthy face had closed in on itself, exposing the loosening sutures around his temples. During the hours of violence in the apartment he had gripped his pistol as if masturbating himself to a continuous orgasm. The torment inflicted upon this elderly diplomat had clearly served a purpose known only to Renata and her companions. They had watched the murder with an almost dreamlike calm, as if Heller's deranged cruelty revealed the secret formulas of a new logic, a conceptualized violence that would transform the air disaster and the car crash into events of loving gentleness. Already they planned an ever-more psychotic series of spectacular adventures – the assassination of the visiting party leader, the hijacking of the plutonium convoy, the reprogramming of ULTRAC to destroy the entire commercial and banking system of the West. These women dreamed of World War III like young mothers crooning over their first pregnancies.

THE SIGN OF THE HYPODERMIC

He watched Dr Vanessa's reflection in the window of the control room as she adjusted the electrodes on his scalp. Her uncertain hands, with their tremor of guilt and affection, summed up all the uncertainties of this dangerous experiment conducted in the converted television studios. Despite Professor Rotblat's disapproval, she had become a willing conspirator, perhaps out of some confused hope that he would make his escape, embark from the causeways of his own spinal column and fly away across some interior sky. The television director's face swam through the heavy glass of the control room. During the previous days, as they set up the experiment in the studio laboratory, Tarrant had begun to hide behind these transparent mirrors, as if uncertain of his own reality. Yet he seemed to sympathize with the need to come to terms with this nightmare world of terrorists and cruise missiles, objects seen in a deformed mirror that might one day be reunited in a more meaningful sequence. Multiplied by the ULTRAC computer, the wave-functions of his hallucinating brain would be transmitted on the nationwide channels and provide a new set of operating formulae for their passage through consciousness. He touched Dr Vanessa's knee reassuringly as she held the hypodermic to the light.

THE SIGN OF THE VIBRATOR

He listened to the monotonous, insect-like buzz of the elegant machine in Renata's hand. She lay on her back, muttering some complex masturbatory fantasy to herself, for once unaware of his presence. Was she really convinced by these

73

shudders and gasps of her own sexual fulfilment? Since his return to her apartment he had often reflected that sex offered to any would-be tyrant the easiest and most effective means of political take-over. However, he had made his own choice elsewhere. Within a few days the terrorist groups would attempt to start World War III, and the psychological year would move to its climax. Already the subliminal films were ready to be transmitted through the emergency news bulletins. Relaxed now, he looked down at Renata's straining thighs and pelvis. By the time the television transmission of this exhausting sex act had reached the nearest stars any curious observers there would assume that she was giving birth to this unpleasant machine, offspring of her marriage with the ULTRAC print-outs.

THE SIGN OF THE CRUISE MISSILE

He knelt in front of the television set, waiting for the overdue emergency bulletins. By now the skies over central London should have been filled with helicopters, the streets deafened by the treads of armoured troop carriers, the whole panoply of nuclear alert. Waiting patiently, confident that the logic of the new zodiac would be fulfilled, he stared at the silent screen as Renata lay asleep on the bed. Deep in his mind he dreamed of cruise missiles, launched from the surfacing submarines and heading out across the lonely tundra, following the contours of remote arctic fjords. Soon he would be leaving, glad to abandon this planet to its nightmare games. He had played only a small part in this reductive drama. The true zodiac of these people, the constellations of their mental skies, constituted nothing more than a huge self-destructive machine. Leaving the set, he looked down at the young woman. As he placed his hands around her neck, ready to satisfy the faultless logic of the psychological round, he was thinking only of the cruise missiles.

THE SIGN OF THE ASTRONAUT

Through the glass window of the isolation ward he watched Dr Vanessa speaking quietly to Professor Rotblat. Her nervous anxiety when the police returned him to the hospital had given way to no more than a neutral and professional concern. He pressed his elbows against the restraining sheet, thinking of Renata's bloodied body, with its strangely resistant anatomy that he had tried to arrange into a happier and more meaningful geometry. He knew now that he had been tricked by them all, that there had been no nuclear crisis, and that the subliminal messages had been intended only for himself. Had it all been no more than a fantasy, and was the search for the zodiac imposed upon him unintentionally by his too-sudden release from the hospital? However, Renata's body remained more than a small clinical embarrassment. One day the murder of this intellectual woman gangster might really seed their society's destruction. He had been trapped by the zodiac they had urged him to construct, but he had escaped through the side door of this young woman's death. The great round had come full circle, raised him on its shoulder and returned him to the institution. However, they had made no allowance for a wholly unexpected contingency – his recovery of his sanity, a treasure abducted from the twelve mansions. Now he would leave them, and take the left-handed staircase to the roof above his mind, and fly away across the free skies of his inner space.

News from the Sun

In the evenings, as Franklin rested on the roof of the abandoned clinic, he would often remember Trippett, and the last drive he had taken into the desert with the dying astronaut and his daughter. On impulse he had given in to the girl's request, when he found her waiting for him in the dismantled laboratory, her father's flight jacket and solar glasses in her hands, shabby mementoes of the vanished age of space. In many ways it had been a sentimental gesture, but Trippett was the last man to walk on the moon, and the untended landscape around the clinic more and more resembled the lunar terrain. Under that cyanide-blue sky perhaps something would stir, a lost memory engage, for a few moments Trippet might even feel at home again.

Followed by the daughter, Franklin entered the darkened ward. The other patients had been transferred, and Trippett sat alone in the wheelchair at the foot of his bed. By now, on the eve of the clinic's closure, the old astronaut had entered his terminal phase and was conscious for only a few seconds each day. Soon he would lapse into his last deep fugue, an invisible dream of the great tideways of space.

Franklin lifted the old man from his chair, and carried his child-like body through the corridors to the car-park at the rear of the clinic. Already, however, as they moved into the needle-sharp sunlight, Franklin regretted his decision, aware that he had been manipulated by the young woman. Ursula rarely spoke to Franklin, and like everyone at the hippy commune seemed to have all the time in the world to stare at him. But her patient, homely features and uninnocent gaze disturbed him in a curious way. Sometimes he suspected that he had kept Trippett at the clinic simply so that he could see the daughter. The younger doctors thought of her as dumpy and unsexed, but Franklin was sure that her matronly body concealed a sexual conundrum of a special kind.

These suspicions aside, her father's condition reminded Franklin of his own accelerating fugues. For a year these had lasted little more than a few minutes each day, manageable within the context of the hours he spent at his desk, and at times barely distinguishable from musing. But in the past few weeks, as if prompted by the decision to close the clinic, they had lengthened to more than thirty minutes at a stretch. In three months he would be housebound, in six be fully awake for only an hour each day.

The fugues came so swiftly, time poured in a torrent from the cracked glass of their lives. The previous summer, during their first excursions into the desert, Trippett's waking periods had lasted at least half an hour. He had taken a touching pleasure in the derelict landscape, in the abandoned motels and weed-choked swimming-pools of the small town near the air base, in the silent runways with their dusty jets sitting on flattened tyres, in the over-bright hills waiting with the infinite guile of the geological kingdom for the organic world to end and a more vivid mineral realm to begin.

Now, sadly, the old astronaut was unaware of all this. He sat beside Franklin in the front seat, his blanched eyes open behind the glasses but his mind set to some private time. Even the motion of the speeding car failed to rouse him, and Ursula had to hold his shoulders as he tottered like a stuffed toy into the windshield.

'Go on, doctor — he likes the speed…' Sitting forward, she tapped Franklin's head, wide eyes fixed on the speedometer. Franklin forced himself to concentrate on the road, conscious of the girl's breath on his neck. This highway madonna, with her secret dream of speed, he found it difficult to keep his hands and mind off her. Was she planning to abduct her father from the clinic? She lived in the small commune that had taken over the old solar city up in the hills, Soleri II. Every morning she cycled in, bringing Trippett his ration of raisins and macrobiotic cheer. She sat calmly beside him like his young mother as he played with the food, making strange patterns on his paper plate.

'Faster, Dr Franklin – I've watched you drive. You're always speeding.'

'So you've seen me? I'm not sure. If I had a blackout now…' Giving in again, Franklin steered the Mercedes into the centre of the road and eased the speedometer needle towards fifty. There was a flare of headlights as they overtook the weekly bus to Las Vegas, a medley of warning shouts from the passengers left behind in a tornado of dust. The Mercedes was already moving at more than twice the legal limit. At twenty miles an hour, theoretically, a driver entering a sudden fugue had time to pass the controls to the obligatory front-seat passenger. In fact, few people drove at all. The desert on either side of the road was littered with the wrecks of cars that had veered off the soft shoulder and ended up in a sand-hill a mile away, their drivers dying of exposure before they could wake from their fugues.

Yet, for all the danger, Franklin loved to drive, illicit high-speed runs at dusk when he seemed to be alone on a forgotten planet. In a locked hangar at the air base were a Porsche and an antique Jaguar. His colleagues at the clinic disapproved, but he pursued his own maverick way, as he did in the laboratory, shielding himself behind a front of calculated eccentricity that excused certain obsessions with speed, time, sex… He needed the speed more than the sex now. But soon he would have to stop, already the fast driving had become a dangerous game spurred on by the infantile hope that speed in some way would keep the clock hands turning.

The concrete towers and domes of the solar city approached on their left, Paulo Soleri's charming fantasy of a self-sufficient community. Franklin slowed to avoid running down a young woman in a sari who stood like a mannequin in the centre of the highway. Her eyes stared at the dust, a palaeontology of hopes. In an hour she would snap out of it, and complete her walk to the bus stop without realizing that time, and the bus, had passed her by.

Ursula sombrely embraced her father, beckoning Franklin to accelerate.

'We're dawdling, doctor. What's the matter? You enjoyed the speed. And so did Dad.'

'Ursula, he doesn't even know he's here.'

Franklin looked out at the desert, trying to imagine it through Trippett's eyes. The landscape was not so much desolate as derelict – the untended irrigation canals, the rusting dish of a radio-telescope on a nearby peak, a poor man's begging bowl held up to the banquet of the universe. The hills were waiting for them to go away. A crime had been committed, a cosmic misdemeanour carried on the shoulders of this fine old astronaut sitting beside him. Every night Trippett wept in his sleep. Spectres strode through his unlit dreams, trying to find a way out of his head.

The best astronauts, Franklin had noticed during his work for NASA, never dreamed. Or, at least, not until ten years after their flights, when the nightmares began and they returned to the institutes of aviation medicine which had first helped to recruit them.

Light flickered at them from the desert, and raced like a momentary cathode trace across the black lenses of Trippett's glasses. Thousands of steel mirrors were laid out in a semi-circular tract beside the road, one of the solar farms that would have provided electric current for the inhabitants of Soleri II, unlimited power donated in a perhaps too kindly gesture by the economy of the sun.

Watching the reflected light dance in Trippett's eyes, Franklin turned the car on to the service road that ran down to the farm.

'Ursula, we'll rest here – I think I'm more tired than your father.'

Franklin stepped from the car, and strolled across the white, calcinated soil towards the nearest of the mirrors. In his eye he followed the focal lines that converged on to the steel tower two hundred feet away. A section of the collector dish had fallen on to the ground, but Franklin could see images of himself flung up into the sky, the outstretched sleeves of his white jacket like the wings of a deformed bird.

'Ursula, bring your father...' The old astronaut could once again see himself suspended in space, this time upside down in the inverted image, hung by his heels from the yard-arm of the sky.

Surprised by the perverse pleasure he took in this notion, Franklin walked back to the car. But as they helped Trippett from his seat, trying to reassure the old man, there was a clatter of metallic noise across the desert. An angular shadow flashed over their faces, and a small aircraft soared past, little more than twenty feet above the ground. It scuttled along like a demented gnat, minute engine buzzing up a storm, its wired wings strung around an open fuselage.

A white-haired man sat astride the miniature controls, naked except for the aviator's goggles tied around his head. He handled the plane in an erratic but stylish way, exploiting the sky to display his showy physique.

Ursula tried to steady her father, but the old man broke away from her and tottered off among the mirrors, his clenched fists pummelling the air. Seeing him, the pilot banked steeply around the sun-tower, then dived straight towards him, pulling up at the last moment in a blare of noise and dust. As Franklin ran forward and pressed Trippett to the ground the plane banked and came round again in a wide turn. The pilot steered the craft with his bare knees, arms trailing at his sides as if mimicking Franklin's image in the dish above the tower.

'Slade! Calm down, for once...' Franklin wiped the stinging grit from his mouth. He had seen the man up to too many extravagant tricks ever to be sure what he would do next. This former air force pilot and would-be astronaut, whose application Franklin had rejected three years earlier when he was chairman of the medical appeals board, had now returned to plague him with these absurd antics – spraying flocks of swallows with gold paint, erecting a circle of towers out in the desert ('my private space programme,' he termed it proudly), building a cargo cult airport with wooden control tower and planes in the air base car-park, a cruel parody intended to punish the few remaining servicemen.

And this incessant stunt flying. Had Slade recognized Franklin's distant reflection as he sped across the desert in the inverted aircraft, then decided to buzz the Mercedes for the fun of it, impress Trippett and Ursula, even himself, perhaps?

The plane was coming back at them, engine wound up to a scream. Franklin saw Ursula shouting at him soundlessly. The old astronaut was shaking like an unstuffed scarecrow, one hand pointing to the mirrors. Reflected in the metal panes were the multiple images of the black aircraft, hundreds of vulture-like birds that hungrily circled the ground.

'Ursula, into the car!' Franklin took off his jacket and ran through the mirrors, hoping to draw the aircraft away from Trippett. But Slade had decided to land. Cutting the engine, he let the microlight die in the air, then stalled the flapping machine on to the service road. As it trundled towards the Mercedes with its still spinning propeller, Franklin held off the starboard wing, almost tearing the doped fabric.

'Doctor! You've already grounded me once too often...'

Slade inspected the dented fabric, then pointed to Franklin's trembling fingers. 'Those hands...I hope you aren't allowed to operate on your patients.'

Franklin looked down at the white-haired pilot. His own hands *were* shaking, an understandable reflex of alarm. For all Slade's ironic drawl, his naked body was as taut as a trap, every muscle tense with hostility. His eyes surveyed Franklin with the ever-alert but curiously dead gaze of a psychopath. His pallid skin was almost luminous, as if after ending his career as an astronaut he had made some private pact with the sun. A narrow lap belt held him to the seat, but his shoulders bore the scars of a strange harness – the restraining straps of a psychiatric unit, Franklin guessed, or some kind of sexual fetishism.

'My hands, yes. They're always the first to let me down. You'll be glad to hear that I retire this week.' Quietly, Franklin added: 'I didn't ground you.'

Slade pondered this, shaking his head. 'Doctor, you practically closed the entire space programme down single-handed. It must have provoked you in a special way. Don't worry, though, I've started my own space programme now, another one.' He pointed to Trippett, who was being soothed by Ursula in the car. 'Why are you still bothering the old man? He won't buy off any unease.'

'He enjoys the drives – speed seems to do him good. And you too, I take it. Be careful of those fugues. If you want to, visit me at the clinic.'

'Franklin...' Controlling his irritation, Slade carefully relaxed his jaw and mouth, as if dismantling an offensive weapon. 'I don't have the fugues any longer. I found a way of...dealing with them.'

'All this flying around? You frightened the old boy.'

'I doubt it.' He watched Trippett nodding to himself. 'In fact, I'd like to take him with me – we'll fly out into space again, one day. Just for him I'll build a gentle space craft, made of rice paper and bamboo...'

82

'That sounds your best idea yet.'

'It is.' Slade stared at Franklin with sudden concern and the almost boyish smile of a pupil before a favourite teacher. 'There is a way out, doctor, a way out of time.'

'Show me, Slade. I haven't much time left.'

'I know that, doctor. That's what I wanted to tell you. Together, Marion and I are going to help you.'

'Marion — ?' But before Franklin could speak, the aircraft's engine racketed into life. Fanning the tailplane, Slade deftly turned the craft within its own length. He replaced the goggles over his eyes, and took off in a funnel of dust that blanched the paintwork of the Mercedes. Safely airborne, he made a final circuit, gave a curious underhand salute and soared away.

Franklin walked to the car and leaned against the roof, catching his breath. The old man was quiet again, his brief fit forgotten.

'That was Slade. Do you know him, Ursula?'

'Everyone does. Sometimes he works on our computer at Soleri, or just starts a fight. He's a bit crazy, trying all the time not to fugue.'

Franklin nodded, watching the plane disappear towards Las Vegas, lost among the hotel towers. 'He was a trainee astronaut once. My wife thinks he's trying to kill me.'

'Perhaps she's right. I remember now — he said that except for you he would have gone to the moon.'

'We all went to the moon. That was the trouble ...'

Franklin reversed the Mercedes along the service road. As they set off along the highway he thought of Slade's puzzling reference to Marion. It was time to be wary. Slade's fugues should have been lengthening for months, yet somehow he kept them at bay. All that violent energy contained in his skull would one day push apart the sutures, burst out in some ugly act of revenge ...

'Dr Franklin! Listen!'

Franklin felt Ursula's hands on his shoulder. In a panic he

slowed down and began to search the sky for the returning microlight.

'It's Dad, doctor! Look!'

The old man had sat up, and was peering through the window in a surprisingly alert way. The slack musculature of his face had drilled itself into the brisk profile of a sometime naval officer. He seemed uninterested in his daughter or Franklin, but stared sharply at a threadbare palm tree beside a wayside motel, and at the tepid water in the partly drained pool.

As the car swayed across the camber Trippett nodded to himself, thoroughly approving of the whole arid landscape. He took his daughter's hand, emphasizing some conversational point that had been interrupted by a pot-hole.

'...it's green here, more like Texas than Nevada. Peaceful, too. Plenty of cool trees and pasturage, all these fields and sweet lakes. I'd like to stop and sleep for a while. We'll come out and swim, dear, perhaps tomorrow. Would you like that?'

He squeezed his daughter's hand with sudden affection. But before he could speak again, a door closed within his face and he had gone.

They reached the clinic and returned Trippett to his darkened ward. Later, while Ursula cycled away down the silent runways, Franklin sat at his desk in the dismantled laboratory. His fingers sparred with each other as he thought of Trippett's curious utterance. In some way Slade's appearance in the sky had set it off. The old astronaut's brief emergence into the world of time, those few lucid seconds, gave him hope. Was it possible that the fugues could be reversed? He was tempted to go back to the ward, and bundle Trippett into the car for another drive.

Then he remembered Slade's aircraft speeding towards him across the solar mirrors, the small, vicious propeller that shredded the light and air, time and space. This failed astronaut had first come to the clinic seven months earlier. While Franklin was away at a conference, Slade arrived by air force ambulance, posing as a terminal patient. With his white hair and obsessive gaze, he had instantly charmed the clinic's director, Dr Rachel Vaisey, into giving him the complete run of the place. Moving about the laboratories and corridors, Slade took over any disused cupboards and desk drawers, where he constructed a series of little tableaux, psychosexual shrines to the strange gods inside his head.

He built the first of the shrines in Rachel Vaisey's bidet, an ugly assemblage of hypodermic syringes, fractured sunglasses and blood-stained tampons. Other shrines appeared in corridor alcoves and unoccupied beds, relics of a yet to be experienced future left here as some kind of psychic deposit against his treatment's probable failure. After an outraged Dr Vaisey insisted on a thorough inspection Slade discharged himself from the clinic and made a new home in the sky.

The shrines were cleared away, but one alone had been carefully preserved. Franklin opened the centre drawer of his desk and stared at the assemblage laid out like a corpse on its bier of surgical cotton. There was a labelled fragment of lunar rock stolen from the NASA museum in Houston; a photograph taken with a zoom lens of Marion in a hotel bathroom, her white body almost merging into the tiles of the shower stall; a faded reproduction of Dali's *Persistence of Memory*, with its soft watches and expiring embryo; a set of leucotomes whose points were masked by metal peas; and an emergency organ-donor card bequeathing to anyone in need his own brain. Together the items formed an accurate anti-portrait of all Franklin's obsessions, a side-chapel of his head. But Slade had always been a keen observer, more interested in Franklin than in anyone else.

How did he elude the fugues? When Franklin had last

seen him at the clinic Slade was already suffering from fugues that lasted an hour or more. Yet somehow he had sprung a trapdoor in Trippett's mind, given him his vision of green fields.

When Rachel Vaisey called to complain about the unauthorized drive Franklin brushed this aside. He tried to convey his excitement over Trippett's outburst.

'He was there, Rachel, completely himself, for something like thirty seconds. And there was no effort involved, no need to remember who he was. It's frightening to think that I'd given him up for lost.'

'It is strange – one of those inexplicable remissions. But try not to read too much into it.' Dr Vaisey stared with distaste at the perimeter camera mounted beside its large turntable. Like most members of her staff, she was only too glad that the clinic was closing, and that the few remaining patients would soon be transferred to some distant sanatorium or memorial home. Within a month she and her colleagues would return to the universities from which they had been seconded. None of them had yet been affected by the fugues, and that Franklin should be the only one to succumb seemed doubly cruel, confirming all their longstanding suspicions about this wayward physician. Franklin had been the first of the NASA psychiatrists to identify the time-sickness, to have seen the astronauts' original fugues for what they were.

Sobered by the prospect facing Franklin, she managed a conciliatory smile. 'You say he spoke coherently. What did he talk about?'

'He babbled of green fields.' Franklin stood behind his desk, staring at the open drawer hidden from Dr Vaisey's suspicious gaze. 'I'm sure he actually saw them.'

'A childhood memory? Poor man, at least he seems happy, wherever he really is.'

'Rachel...!' Franklin drove the drawer into the desk. 'Trippett was staring at the desert along the road – nothing but rock, dust and a few dying palms, yet he saw green fields, lakes, forests of trees. We've got to keep the clinic open a little longer, I feel I have a chance now. I want to go back to the beginning and think everything through again.'

Before Dr Vaisey could stop him, Franklin had started to pace the floor, talking to his desk. 'Perhaps the fugues are a preparation for something, and we've been wrong to fear them. The symptoms are so widespread, there's virtually an invisible epidemic, one in a hundred of the population involved, probably another five unaware that they've been affected, certainly out here in Nevada.'

'It's the desert – topography clearly plays a part in the fugues. It's been bad for you, Robert. For all of us.'

'All the more reason to stay and face it. Rachel, listen: I'm willing to work with the others more than I have done, this time we'll be a true team.'

'That is a concession.' Dr Vaisey spoke without irony. 'But too late, Robert. You've tried everything.'

'I've tried nothing...' Franklin placed a hand on the huge lens of the perimeter camera, hiding the deformed figure who mimicked his gestures from the glass cell. Distorted reflections of himself had pursued him all day, as if he were being presented with brief clips from an obscene film in which he would shortly star. If only he had spent more time on Trippett, rather than on the volunteer panels of housewives and air force personnel. But the old astronaut intimidated him, touched all his feelings of guilt over his complicity in the space programme. As a member of the medical support team, he had helped to put the last astronauts into space, made possible the year-long flights that had set off the whole time-plague, cracked the cosmic hour-glass...

'And Trippett? Where are you going to hide him away?'

'We aren't. His daughter has volunteered to take him. She seems a reasonable girl.'

Giving in to her concern, Dr Vaisey stepped forward and

took Franklin's hand from the camera lens. 'Robert – are you going to be all right? Your wife will look after you, you say. I wish you'd let me meet her. I could insist…'

Franklin was thinking about Trippett – the news that the old astronaut would still be there, presumably living up in Soleri II, had given him hope. The work could go on…

He felt a sudden need to be alone in the empty clinic, to be rid of Dr Vaisey, this well-meaning, middle-aged neurologist with her closed mind and closed world. She was staring at him across the desk, clearly unsure what to do about Franklin, her eyes distracted by the gold and silver swallows that swooped across the runways. Dr Vaisey had always regretted her brief infatuation with Slade. Franklin remembered their last meeting in her office, when Slade had taken out his penis and masturbated in front of her, then insisted on mounting his hot semen on a slide. Through the microscope eyepiece Rachel Vaisey had watched the thousand replicas of this young psychotic frantically swimming. After ten minutes they began to falter. Within an hour they were all dead.

'Don't worry, I'll be fine. Marion knows exactly what I need. And Slade will be around to help her.'

'Slade? How on earth…?'

Franklin eased the centre drawer from his desk. Carefully, as if handling an explosive device, he offered the shrine to Dr Vaisey's appalled gaze.

'Take it, Rachel. It's the blueprint of our joint space programme. You might care to come along…'

When Dr Vaisey had gone, Franklin returned to his desk. First, he took off his wristwatch and massaged the raw skin of his forearm. Every fifteen minutes he returned the hand of the stop-watch to zero. This nervous tic, a time-twitch, had long been a joke around the clinic. But after the onset of a fugue the accumulating total gave him a reasonably exact record of its duration. A crude device, he was almost glad that he would soon escape from time altogether.

Though not yet. Calming himself, he looked at the last pages of his diary.

June 19 – fugues: 8-30 to 9-11 am; 11-45 to 12-27 am; 5-15 to 6-08 pm; 11-30 to 12-14 pm. Total: 3 hours.

The totals were gaining on him. June 20 – 3 hours 14 mins; June 21 – 3 hours 30 mins; June 22 – 3 hours 46 mins. This gave him little more than ten weeks, unless the fugues began to slow down, or he found that trapdoor through which Trippett had briefly poked his head.

Franklin closed the diary and stared back at the watching lens of the perimeter camera. Curiously, he had never allowed himself to be photographed by the machine, as if the contours of his body constituted a secret terrain whose codes had to be held in reserve for his last attempt to escape. Standing or reclining on the rotating platform, the volunteer patients had been photographed in a continuous scan that transformed them into a landscape of undulating hills and valleys, not unlike the desert outside. Could they take an aerial photograph of the Sahara and Gobi deserts, reverse the process and reconstitute the vast figure of some sleeping goddess, an Aphrodite born from a sea of dunes? Franklin had become obsessed with the camera, photographing everything from cubes and spheres to cups and saucers and then the naked patients themselves, in the hope of finding the dimension of time locked in those undulating spaces.

The volunteers had long since retired to their terminal wards, but their photographs were still pinned to the walls – a retired dentist, a police sergeant on the Las Vegas force, a middle-aged hair stylist, an attractive mother of year-old twins, an air-traffic controller from the base. Their splayed features and distorted anatomies resembled the nightmarish jumble seen by all patients if they were deliberately roused from their fugues by powerful stimulants or electric shock – oozing forms in an elastic world, giddying and unpleasant. Without time, a moving face seemed to smear itself across the air, the human body became a surrealist monster.

For Franklin, and the tens of thousands of fellow sufferers, the fugues had begun in the same way, with the briefest moments of inattention. An overlong pause in the middle of a sentence, some mysteriously burnt-out scrambled egg, the air force sergeant who looked after the Mercedes annoyed by his off-hand rudeness, together led on to longer stretches of missed time. Subjectively, the moment to moment flow of consciousness seemed to be uninterrupted. But time drained away, leaking slowly from his life. Only the previous day he had been standing at the window, looking at the line of cars in the late afternoon sunlight, and the next moment there was dusk outside and a deserted parking lot.

All victims told the same story – there were forgotten appointments, inexplicable car crashes, untended infants rescued by police and neighbours. The victims would 'wake' at midnight in empty office blocks, find themselves in stagnant baths, be arrested for jay-walking, forget to feed themselves. Within six months they would be conscious for only half the day, afraid to drive or go out into the streets, desperately filling every room with clocks and timepieces. A week would flash past in a jumble of sunsets and dawns. By the end of the first year they would be alert for only a few minutes each day, no longer able to feed or care for themselves, and soon after would enter one of the dozens of state hospitals and sanatoria.

After his arrival at the clinic Franklin's first patient was a badly burned fighter pilot who had taxied his jet through the doors of a hangar. The second was one of the last of the astronauts, a former naval captain named Trippett. The pilot was soon beyond reach in a perpetual dusk, but Trippett had hung on, lucid for a few minutes each day. Franklin had learned a great deal from Trippett, the last man to have walked on the moon and the last to hold out against the fugues – all the early astronauts had long since retreated into a timeless world. The hundreds of fragmentary conversations, and the mysterious guilt that Trippett shared with his colleagues, like them weeping in his dreams, convinced Franklin that the sources of the malaise were to be found in the space programme itself.

By leaving his planet and setting off into outer space man had committed an evolutionary crime, a breach of the rules governing his tenancy of the universe, and of the laws of time and space. Perhaps the right to travel through space belonged to another order of beings, but his crime was being punished just as surely as would be any attempt to ignore the laws of gravity. Certainly the unhappy lives of the astronauts bore all the signs of a deepening sense of guilt. The relapse into alcoholism, silence and pseudo-mysticism, and the mental breakdowns, suggested profound anxieties about the moral and biological rightness of space exploration.

Sadly, not only the astronauts were affected. Each space-launch left its trace in the minds of those watching the expeditions. Each flight to the moon and each journey around the sun was a trauma that warped their perception of time and space. The brute-force ejection of themselves from their planet had been an act of evolutionary piracy, for which they were now being expelled from the world of time.

Preoccupied with his memories of the astronauts, Franklin was the last to leave the clinic. He had expected his usual afternoon fugue, and sat at his desk in the silent laboratory, finger on his stop-watch. But the fugue had not occurred, perhaps deflected by his buoyant mood after the drive with Trippett. As he walked across the car-park he looked out over the deserted air base. Two hundred yards from the control tower, a young woman with an apron around her waist stood on the concrete runway, lost in her fugue. Half a mile away, two more women stood in the centre of the huge cargo runway. All of them came from the nearby town. At twilight these women of the runways left their homes and trailers and strayed across the air base, staring into the dusk like the wives of forgotten astronauts waiting for their husbands to return from the tideways of space.

The sight of these women always touched Franklin in a disturbing way, and he had to force himself to start the car. As he drove towards Las Vegas the desert seemed almost lunar in the evening light. No one came to Nevada now, and most of the local population had long since left, fearing the uneasy perspectives of the desert. When he reached home the dusk filtered through a cerise haze that lay over the old casinos and hotels, a ghostly memory of the electric night.

Franklin liked the abandoned gambling resort. The other physicians lived within a short drive of the clinic, but Franklin had chosen one of the half-empty motels in the northern suburbs of the city. In the evenings, after visiting his few patients in their retirement homes, he would often drive down the silent Strip, below the sunset façades of the vast hotels, and wander for hours through the shadows among the drained swimming-pools. This city of spent dreams, which had once boasted that it contained no clocks, now seemed itself to be in fugue.

As he parked in the forecourt of the motel he noted that Marion's car was missing. The third-floor apartment was empty. The television set was drawn up by the bed, playing silently to a clutch of medical textbooks Marion had taken from his shelves and an overflowing ashtray like a vent of Vesuvius. Franklin hung the unracked dresses in the wardrobe. As he counted the fresh cigarette burns in the carpet he reflected on the remarkable disarray that Marion could achieve in a few hours, here as in everything else. Were her fugues real or simulated? Sometimes he suspected that she half-consciously mimicked the time-slips, in an effort to enter that one realm where Franklin was free of her, safe from all her frustration at having come back to him.

Franklin went on to the balcony and glanced down at the empty swimming-pool. Often Marion sunbathed nude on the floor at the deep end, and perhaps had been trapped there by her fugue. He listened to the drone of a light aircraft circling the distant hotels, and learned from the retired geologist in the next apartment that Marion had driven away only minutes before his arrival.

As he set off in the car he realized that his afternoon fugue had still not occurred. Had Marion seen his headlamps approaching across the desert, and then decided on impulse to disappear into the unlit evening of the Strip hotels? She had known Slade at Houston three years earlier, when he tried to persuade her to intercede with Franklin. Now he seemed to be courting her from the sky, for reasons that Marion probably failed to realize. Even their original affair had been part of his elaborate stalking of Franklin.

The aircraft had vanished, disappearing across the desert. Franklin drove along the Strip, turning in and out of the hotel forecourts. In an empty car-park he saw one of the ghosts of the twilight, a middle-aged man in a shabby tuxedo, some retired croupier or cardiologist returning to these dreaming hulks. Caught in mid-thought, he stared sightlessly at a dead neon sign. Not far away, a strong-hipped young woman stood among the dusty pool-furniture, her statuesque figure transformed by the fugue into that of a Delvaux muse.

Franklin stopped to help them, if possible rouse them before they froze in the cold desert night. But as he stepped from his car he saw that the headlamps were reflected in the stationary propeller blade of a small aircraft parked on the Strip.

Slade leaned from the cockpit of his microlight, his white skin an unhealthy ivory in the electric beams. He was still naked, gesturing in an intimate way at a handsome woman in a streetwalker's fur who was playfully inspecting his cockpit. He beckoned her towards the narrow seat, like some cruising driver of old trying to entice a passer-by.

Admiring Slade for his nerve in using the sky to accost his wife, Franklin broke into a run. Slade had taken Marion's waist and was trying to pull her into the cockpit.

'Leave her, Slade!' Fifty feet from them, Franklin stumbled over a discarded tyre. He stopped to catch his breath as – an engine of noise hurtled towards him out of the darkness, the same metallic blare he had heard in the desert that morning. Slade's aircraft raced along the Strip, wheels bouncing on the road, its propeller lit by the car's headlamps. As Franklin fell to his knees the plane banked to avoid him, climbed steeply and soared away into the sky.

Hunting for Slade, the excited air surged around Franklin. He stood up, hands raised to shield his face from the stinging dust. The darkness was filled with rotating blades. Silver lassoes spiralled out of the night, images of the propeller that launched themselves one after another from the wake of the vanished aircraft.

Still stunned by the violent attack of the machine, Franklin listened to its last drone across the desert. He watched the retinal display that had transformed the shadowy streets. Silver coils spun away over his head and disappeared among the hotels, a glistening flight path that he could almost touch with his hands. Steadying himself against the hard pavement under his feet, he turned to follow his wife as she fled from him through the drained swimming-pools and deserted car-parks of the newly-lit city.

'Poor man – couldn't you see him? He flew straight at you. Robert … ?'

'Of course I saw him. I don't think I'd be here otherwise.'

'But you stood there, totally mesmerized. I know he's always fascinated you, but that was carrying it too far. If that propeller had…'

'It was a small experiment,' Franklin said. 'I wanted to see what he was trying to do.'

'He was trying to kill you!'

Franklin sat on the end of the bed, staring at the cigarette burns in the carpet. They had reached the apartment fifteen minutes earlier, but he was still trying to calm himself. He thought of the rotating blade that had devoured the darkness. Delayed all afternoon, his fugue had begun as he tripped over the tyre, and had lasted almost an hour. For her own reasons Marion was pretending that the fugue had not occurred, but when he woke his skin was frozen. What had she and Slade been doing during the lost time? Too easily, Franklin imagined them together in Marion's car, or even in the cockpit of the aircraft, watched by the sightless husband. That would please Slade, put him in just the mood to scare the wits out of Franklin as he took off.

Through the open door Franklin stared at his wife's naked body in the white cube of the bathroom. A wet cigarette smouldered in the soap dish. There were clusters of small bruises on her thighs and hips, marks of some stylized grapple. One day soon, when the time drained out of her, the contours of her breasts and thighs would migrate to the polished walls, calm as the dunes and valleys of the perimeter photographs.

Sitting down at the dressing-table, Marion peered over her powdered shoulder with some concern. 'Are you going to be all right? I'm finding it difficult enough to cope with myself. That wasn't an attack…?'

'Of course not.' For months now they had kept up the pretence that neither of them was affected by the fugues. Marion needed the illusion, more in Franklin's case than in her own. 'But I may not always be immune.'

'Robert, if anyone's immune, you are. Think of yourself,

what you've always wanted – alone in the world, just you and these empty hotels. But be careful of Slade.'

'I am.' Casually, Franklin added: 'I want you to see more of him. Arrange a meeting.'

'What?' Marion looked round at her husband again, her left contact lens trapped under her eyelid. 'He was naked, you know.'

'So I saw. That's part of his code. Slade's trying to tell me something. He needs me, in a special way.'

'Needs you? He doesn't need you, believe me. But for you he would have gone to the moon. You took that away from him, Robert.'

'And I can give it back to him.'

'How? Are the two of you going to start your own space programme?'

'In a sense we already have. But we really need you to help us.'

Franklin waited for her to reply, but Marion sat raptly in front of the mirror, lens case in one hand, fingers retracting her upper and lower eyelids around the trapped lens. Fused with her own reflection in the finger-stained glass, she seemed to be shooting the sun with a miniature sextant, finding her bearings in this city of empty mirrors. He remembered their last month together after the end at Cape Kennedy, the long drive down the dead Florida coast. The space programme had expressed all its failure in that terminal moraine of deserted hotels and apartment houses, a cryptic architecture like the forgotten codes of a discarded geometric language. He remembered Marion's blood flowing into the hand-basin from her slashed palms, and the constant arguments that warped themselves out of the air.

Yet curiously those had been happy days, filled with the quickening excitements of her illness. He had dreamed of her promiscuity, the deranged favours granted to waitresses and bellboys. He came back alone from Miami, resting beside the swimming-pools of the empty hotels, remembering the intoxications of abandoned parking lots. In a sense that drive had been his first conscious experiment with time and space, placing that body and its unhappy mind in a sequence of bathrooms and pools, watching her with her lovers in the diagrammed car-parks, emotions hung on these abstract webs of space.

Affectionately, Franklin placed his hands on Marion's shoulders, feeling the familiar clammy skin of the fugue. He lowered her hands to her lap, and then removed the contact lens from her eyeball, careful not to cut the cornea. Franklin smiled down at her blanched face, counting the small scars and blemishes that had appeared around her mouth. Like all women, Marion never really feared the fugues, accepting the popular myth that during these periods of lapsed time the body refused to age.

Sitting beside her on the stool, Franklin embraced her gently. He held her breasts in his palms, for a moment shoring up their slipping curvatures. For all his fondness for Marion, he would have to use her in his duel with Slade. The planes of her thighs and shoulders were segments of a secret runway along which he would one day fly to safety.

July 5

Not one of my best days. Five long fugues, each lasting over an hour. The first started at 9 am as I was walking around the pool towards the car. Suddenly I found myself standing by the deep end in much steeper sunlight, the old geologist poking me in a concerned way. Marion had told him not to disturb me, I was deep in thought! I must remember to wear a hat in future, the sunlight brought out a viral rash on my lips. An excuse for Marion not to kiss me, without realizing it she's eager to get away from here, can't pretend for much longer that the fugues don't exist. Does she guess that in some way I plan to exploit that keening sex of hers?

These long fugues are strange, for the first time since

the airplane attack I have a vague memory of the dead time. The geometry of that drained pool acted like a mirror, the sky seemed to be full of suns. Perhaps Marion knew what she was doing when she sunbathed there. I ought to climb down that rusty chromium ladder into a new kind of time? *Lost time total*: 6 hours 50 min.

July 11

A dangerous fugue today, and what may have been another attempt on my life by Slade. I nearly killed myself driving to the clinic, must think hard about going there again. The first fugue came at 8-15 am, synchronized with Marion's – our sole connubial activity now. I must have spent an hour opening the bathroom door, staring at her as she stood motionless in the shower stall. Curious after-images, sections of her anatomy seemed to be splayed across the walls and ceiling, even over the car-park outside. For the first time I felt that it might be possible to stay awake during the fugues. A weird world, spatial change perceived independently of time.

Fired by all this, I set off for the clinic, eager to try something out on the perimeter camera. But only a mile down the highway I must have gone straight off the road, found myself in the parking lot of some abandoned hypermarket, surrounded by a crowd of staring faces. In fact, they were department store mannequins. Suddenly there was a volley of gunshots, fibreglass arms and heads were flying everywhere. Slade at his games again, this time with a pump-gun on the roof of the hypermarket. He must have seen me stranded there and placed the mannequins around me. The timeless people, the only mementoes of *homo sapiens* when we've all gone, waiting here with their idiotic smiles for the first stellar visitor.

How does Slade repress the fugues? Perhaps violence, like pornography, is some kind of evolutionary standby system, a last-resort device for throwing a wild joker into

98

the game? A widespread taste for pornography means that nature is alerting us to some threat of extinction. I keep thinking about Ursula, incidentally... *Total time lost*: 8 hours 17 min.

July 15

Must get out of this motel more often. A curious by-product of the fugues is that I'm losing all sense of urgency. Sat here for the last three days, calmly watching time run through my fingers. Almost convinces me that the fugues are a good thing, a sign that some great biological step forward is about to take place, set off by the space flights. Alternatively, my mind is simply numbing itself through sheer fear...

This morning I forced myself into the sunlight. I drove slowly around Las Vegas, looking out for Marion and thinking about the links between gambling and time. One could devise a random world, where the length of each time interval depended on chance. Perhaps the high-rollers who came to Vegas were nearer the truth than they realized. 'Clock time' is a neurophysiological construct, a measuring rod confined to *homo sapiens*. The old labrador owned by the geologist next door obviously has a different sense of time, likewise the cicadas beside the pool. Even the materials of my body and the lower levels of my brain have a very different sense of time from my cerebrum – that uninvited guest within my skull.

Simultaneity? It's possible to imagine that everything is happening at once, all the events 'past' and 'future' which constitute the universe are taking place together. Perhaps our sense of time is a primitive mental structure that we inherited from our less intelligent forebears. For prehistoric man the invention of time (a brilliant conceptual leap) was a way of classifying and storing the huge flood of events which his dawning mind had opened for him. Like a dog burying a large bone, the invention of time allowed him to postpone the recognition of an event-system too large for him to grasp at one bite.

If time *is* a primitive mental structure we have inherited, then we ought to welcome its atrophy, embrace the fugues — *Total time lost*: 9 hours 15 min.

July 25

Everything is slowing down, I have to force myself to remember to eat and shower. It's all rather pleasant, no fear even though I'm left with only six or seven hours of conscious time each day. Marion comes and goes, we literally have no time to talk to each other. A day passes as quickly as an afternoon. At lunch I was looking at some album photographs of my mother and father, and a formal wedding portrait of Marion and myself, and suddenly it was evening. I feel a strange nostalgia for my childhood friends, as if I'm about to meet them for the first time, an awakening premonition of the past. I can see the past coming alive in the dust on the balcony, in the dried leaves at the bottom of the pool, part of an immense granary of past time whose doors we can open with the right key. Nothing is older than the very new — a newborn baby with its head emerging from its mother has the smooth, time-worn features of Pharaoh. The whole process of life is the discovery of the immanent past contained in the present.

At the same time, I feel a growing nostalgia for the future, a memory of the future I have already experienced but somehow forgotten. In our lives we try to repeat those significant events which have already taken place in the future. As we grow older we feel an increasing nostalgia for our own deaths, through which we have already passed. Equally, we have a growing premonition of our births, which are about to take place. At any moment we may be born for the first time. *Total time lost*: 10 hours 5 min.

July 29

Slade has been here. I suspect that he's been entering the apartment while I fugue. I had an uncanny memory of someone in the bedroom this morning, when I came out of the 11 am fugue there was a curious after-image, almost a pentecostal presence, a vaguely bio-morphic blur that hung in the air like a photograph taken with the perimeter camera. My pistol had been removed from the dressing-table drawer and placed on my pillow. There's a small diagram of white paint on the back of my left hand. Some kind of cryptic pattern, a geometric key.

Has Slade been reading my diary? This afternoon someone painted the same pattern across the canted floor of the swimming-pool and over the gravel in the car-park. Presumably all part of Slade's serious games with time and space. He's trying to rally me, force me out of the apartment, but the fugues leave me with no more than two hours at a stretch of conscious time. I'm not the only one affected. Las Vegas is almost deserted, everyone has retreated indoors. The old geologist and his wife sit all day in their bedroom, each in a straight-backed chair on either side of the bed. I gave them a vitamin shot, but they're so emaciated they won't last much longer. No reply from the police or ambulance services. Marion is away again, hunting the empty hotels of the Strip for any sign of Slade. No doubt she thinks that he alone can save her. *Total time lost*: 12 hours 35 min.

August 12

Rachel Vaisey called today, concerned about me and disappointed not to find Marion here. The clinic has closed, and she's about to go east. A strange pantomime, we talked stiffly for ten minutes. She was clearly baffled by my calm appearance, despite my beard and coffee-stained trousers, and kept staring at the white pattern on my hand and at the similar shapes on the bedroom ceiling, the car-park outside and even a section of a small apartment house half a mile away. I'm now at the focus of a huge geometric puzzle radiating from my left hand through the open window and out across Las Vegas and the desert.

I was relieved when she had gone. Ordinary time – so-called 'real time' – now seems totally unreal. With her discrete existence, her prissy point-to-point consciousness, Rachel reminded me of a figure in an animated tableau of Time Man in an anthropological museum of the future. All the same, it's difficult to be too optimistic. I wish Marion were here. *Total time lost*: 15 hours 7 min.

August 21

Down now to a few stretches of consciousness that last barely an hour at the most. Time seems continuous, but the days go by in a blur of dawns and sunsets. Almost continuously eating, or I'll die of starvation. I only hope that Marion can look after herself, she doesn't seem to have been here for weeks –

– the pen snapped in Franklin's hand. As he woke, he found himself slumped across his diary. Torn pages lay on the carpet around his feet. During the two-hour fugue a violent struggle had taken place, his books were scattered around an overturned lamp, there were heel marks in the cigarette ash on the floor. Franklin touched his bruised shoulders. Someone had seized him as he sat there in his fugue, trying to shake him into life, and had torn the watch from his wrist.

A familiar noise sounded from the sky. The clacking engine of a light aircraft crossed the nearby roof-tops. Franklin stood up, shielding his eyes from the vivid air on the balcony. He watched the aircraft circle the surrounding streets and then speed towards him. A molten light dripped from the propeller, spraying the motel with liquid platinum, a retinal tincture that briefly turned the street dust to silver.

The plane flew past, heading north from Las Vegas, and he saw that Slade had recruited a passenger. A blonde woman in a ragged fur sat behind the naked pilot, hands clasped around his waist. Like a startled dreamer, she stared down at Franklin.

As the microlight soared away, Franklin went into the bathroom. Rallying himself, he gazed at the sallow, bearded figure in the mirror, a ghost of himself. Already sections of his mind were migrating towards the peaceful geometry of the bathroom walls. But at least Marion was still alive. Had she tried to intercede as Slade attacked him? There was a faint image on the air of a wounded woman...

Las Vegas was deserted. Here and there, as he set off in the car, he saw a grey face at a window, or a blanket draped across two pairs of knees on a balcony. All the clocks had stopped, and without his watch he could no longer tell how long the fugues had lasted, or when the next was about to begin.

Driving at a cautious ten miles an hour, Franklin slowed to a halt every five miles, then waited until he found himself sitting in the car with a cold engine. The temperature dial became his clock. It was almost noon when he reached the air base. The clinic was silent, its car-park empty. Weeds grew through the fading marker lines, an empty report sheet left behind by those unhappy psychiatrists and their now vanished patients.

Franklin let himself into the building and walked through the deserted wards and laboratories. His colleagues' equipment had been shipped away, but when he unlocked the doors to his own laboratory he found the packing cases where he had left them.

In front of the perimeter camera a rubber mattress lay on the turntable. Next to it an ashtray overflowed with cigarette ends that had burned the wooden planks.

So Slade had turned his talents to a special kind of photography – a pornography in the round. Pinned to the walls behind the camera was a gallery of huge prints. These strange landscapes resembled aerial photographs of a desert convulsed by a series of titanic earthquakes, as if one geological era were giving birth to another. Elongated clefts and gulleys stretched across the prints, their contours so like those that had lingered in the apartment after Marion's showers.

But a second geometry overlayed the first, a scarred and aggressive musculature he had seen borne on the wind. The aircraft was parked outside the window, its cockpit and passenger seat empty in the sunlight. A naked man sat behind the desk in Franklin's office, goggles around his forehead. Looking at him, Franklin realized why Slade had always appeared naked.

'Come in, doctor. God knows it's taken you long enough to get here.' He weighed Franklin's wristwatch in his hand, clearly disappointed by the shabby figure in front of him. He had removed the centre drawer from the desk, and was playing with Franklin's shrine. To the original objects Slade had added a small chromium pistol. Deciding against the wristwatch, he tossed it into the waste basket.

'I don't think that's really part of you any longer. You're a man without time. I've moved into your office, Franklin. Think of it as my mission control centre.'

'Slade...' Franklin felt a sudden queasiness, a warning of the onset of the next fugue. The air seemed to warp itself around him. Holding the door-frame, he restrained himself from rushing to the waste basket. 'Marion's here with you. I need to see her.'

'See her, then...' Slade pointed to the perimeter photographs. 'I'm sure you recognize her, Franklin. You've been using her for the last ten years. That's why you joined NASA. You've been pilfering from your wife and the agency in the same way, stealing the parts for your space machine. I've even helped you myself.'

'Helped...? Marion told me that –'

'Franklin!' Slade stood up angrily, knocking the chromium pistol on to the floor. His hands worked clumsily at his scarred ribs, as if he were forcing himself to breathe. Watching him, Franklin could almost believe that Slade had held back the fugues by a sheer effort of will, by a sustained anger against the very dimensions of time and space.

'This time, doctor, you can't ground me. But for you I would have walked on the moon!'

Franklin was watching the pistol at his feet, uncertain how to pacify this manic figure. 'Slade, but for me you'd be with the others. If you'd flown with the space-crews you'd be like Trippett.'

'I am like Trippett.' Calm again, Slade stepped to the window and stared at the empty runways. 'I'm taking the old boy, Franklin. He's coming with me to the sun. It's a pity you're not coming. But don't worry, you'll find a way out of the fugues. In fact, I'm relying on it.'

He stepped around the desk and picked the pistol from the floor. As Franklin swayed, he touched the physician's cooling forehead with the weapon. 'I'm going to kill you, Franklin. Not now, but right at the end, as we go out into that last fugue. Trippett and I will be flying to the sun, and you... you'll die forever.'

There were fifteen minutes, at the most, before the next fugue. Slade had vanished, taking the aircraft into the sky. Franklin gazed round the silent laboratory, listening to the empty air. He retrieved his wristwatch from the waste basket and left. As he reached the parking lot, searching for his car among the maze of diagonal lines, the desert landscape around the air base resembled the perimeter photographs of Marion and Slade together. The hills wavered and shimmered, excited echoes of that single sexual act, mimicking every caress.

Already the moisture in his body was being leached away by the sun. His skin prickled with an attack of hives. He left the clinic and drove through the town, slowing to avoid the filling-station proprietor, his wife and child who stood in the centre of the road. They stared sightlessly into the haze as if waiting for the last car in the world.

He set off towards Las Vegas, trying not to look at the surrounding hills. Ravines fondled each other, rock-towers undulated as if the earth itself were on its marriage bed. Irritated by his own sweat and the oozing hills, Franklin urged on the accelerator, pushing the car's speed to forty miles an hour. The whole mineral world seemed intent on taking its revenge on him. Light stabbed at his retinas from the exposed quartz veins, from the rusting bowls of the radar dishes on the hill crests. Franklin fixed his eyes on the speeding marker line between the car's wheels, dreaming of Las Vegas, that dusty Samarkand.

Then time side-stepped in front of him again.

He woke to find himself lying under the torn ceiling liner of the overturned car, his legs stretched through the broken windshield. Burst from their locks, the open doors hung above him in a haze of idle dust. Franklin pushed aside the loose seats that had fallen across him and climbed from the car. A faint steam rose from the fractured radiator, and the last of the coolant trickled into the culvert of the old irrigation system into which the car had slewed. The blue liquid formed a small pool, then, as he watched it, sank into the sand.

A single kite circled the sky over his head, but the landscape was empty. Half a mile away was the tarry strip of the highway. As he fugued the car had veered off the road, then sped in a wide circle across the scrub, upending itself as it jumped the first of the irrigation ditches. Franklin brushed the sand from his face and beard. He had been unconscious for almost two hours, part-concussion and part-fugue, and the harsh, noon light had driven all shadows from the sandy soil. The northern suburbs of Las Vegas were ten miles away, too far for him to walk, but the white domes of Soleri II rose from the foothills to the west of the highway, little more than two miles across the desert. He could see the metallic flicker of the solar mirrors as one of the canted dishes caught the sun.

Still jarred by the crash, Franklin turned his back to the road and set off along the causeway between the irrigation ditches. After only a hundred yards he sank to his knees. The sand liquefied at his feet, sucking at his shoes as if eager to strip the clothes from his back and expose him to the sun.

Playing its private game with Franklin, the sun changed places in the sky. The fugues were coming at fifteen minute intervals. He found himself leaning against a rusting pump-head. Huge pipes emerged thirstlessly from the forgotten ground. His shadow hid behind him, scuttling under his heels. Franklin waved away the circling kite. All too easily he could imagine the bird perching on his shoulder as he fugued, and lunching off his eyes. He was still more than a mile from the solar mirrors, but their sharp light cut at his retinas. If he could reach the tower, climb a few of its steps and signal with a fragment of broken glass, someone might...

...the sun was trying to trick him again. More confident now, his shadow had emerged from beneath his heels and slid silkily along the stony ground, unafraid of this tottering scarecrow who made an ordeal of each step. Franklin sat down in the dust. Lying on his side, he felt the blisters on his eyelids, lymph-filled sacs that had almost closed his orbits. Any more fugues and he would die here, blood, life and time would run out of him at the same moment.

He stood up and steadied himself against the air. The hills undulated around him, the copulating bodies of all the women he had known, together conceiving this mineral world for him to die within.

Three hundred yards away, between himself and the solar mirrors, a single palm tree dipped its green parasol. Franklin stepped gingerly through the strange light, nervous of this mirage. As he moved forward a second palm appeared, then a third and fourth. There was a glimmer of blue water, the calm surface of an oasis pool.

His body had given up, the heavy arms and legs that emerged from his trunk had slipped into the next fugue. But his mind had scrambled free inside his skull. Franklin knew that even if this oasis were a mirage, it was a mirage that he could see, and that for the first time he was conscious during a fugue. Like the driver of a slow-witted automaton, he propelled himself across the sandy ground, a half-roused sleepwalker clinging to the blue pool before his eyes. More trees had appeared, groves of palms lowered their fronds to the glassy surface of a serpentine lake.

Franklin hobbled forward, ignoring the two kites in the sky above his head. The air was engorged with light, a flood of photons crowded around him. A third kite appeared, joined almost at once by half a dozen more.

But Franklin was looking at the green valley spread out in front of him, at the forest of palms that shaded an archipelago of lakes and pools, together fed by cool streams that ran down from the surrounding hills. Everything seemed calm and yet vivid, the young earth seen for the first time, where all Franklin's ills would be soothed and assuaged in its sweet waters. Within this fertile valley everything multiplied itself without effort. From his outstretched arms fell a dozen shadows, each cast by one of the twelve suns above his head.

Towards the end, while he made his last attempt to reach the lake, he saw a young woman walking towards him. She moved through the palm trees with concerned eyes, hands clasped at her waist, as if searching for a child or elderly parent who had strayed into the wilderness. As Franklin waved to her she was joined by her twin, another grave-faced young woman who walked with the same cautious step. Behind them came other sisters, moving through the palms like schoolgirls from their class, concubines from a pavilion cooled by the lake. Kneeling before them, Franklin waited for the women to find him, to take him away from the desert to the meadows of the valley.

Time, in a brief act of kindness, flowed back into Franklin. He lay in a domed room, behind a verandah shaded by a glass awning. Through the railings he could see the towers and apartment terraces of Soleri II, its concrete architecture a reassuring shoulder against the light. An old man sat on a terrace across the square. Although deeply asleep, he remained inwardly alert and gestured with his hands in a rhythmic way, happily conducting an orchestra of stones and creosote bushes.

Franklin was glad to see the old astronaut. All day Trippett sat in his chair, conducting the desert through its repertory of invisible music. Now and then he sipped a little water that Ursula brought him, and then returned to his colloquy with the sun and the dust.

The three of them lived alone in Soleri II, in this empty city of a future without time. Only Franklin's wristwatch and its restless second hand linked them to the past world.

'Doctor Franklin, why don't you throw it away?' Ursula asked him, as she fed Franklin the soup she prepared each morning on the solar fireplace in the piazza. 'You don't need it any more. There's no time to tell.'

'Ursula, I know. It's some kind of link, I suppose, a telephone line left open to a world we're leaving behind. Just in case...'

Ursula raised his head and dusted the sand from his pillow. With only an hour left to her each day, housework played little part in her life. Yet her broad face and hand-

109

some body expressed all the myths of the maternal child. She had seen Franklin wandering across the desert as she sat on her verandah during an early afternoon fugue.

'I'm sorry I couldn't find you, doctor. There were hundreds of you, the desert was covered with dying men, like some kind of lost army. I didn't know which one to pick.'

'I'm glad you came, Ursula. I saw you as a crowd of dreamy schoolgirls. There's so much to learn...'

'You've made a start, doctor. I knew it months ago when we drove Dad out here. There's enough time.'

They both laughed at this, as the old man across the piazza conducted the orchestral sands. Enough time, when time was what they were most eager to escape. Franklin held the young woman's wrist and listened to her calm pulse, impatient for the next fugue to begin. He looked out over the arid valley below, at the cloud-filled mirrors of the solar farm and the rusting tower with its cracked collector dish. Where were those groves of palms and magic lakes, the sweet streams and pastures from which the grave and beautiful young women had emerged to carry him away to safety? During the fugues that followed his recovery they had begun to return, but not as vividly as he had seen them from the desert floor in the hours after his crash. Each fugue, though, gave him a glimpse of that real world, streams flowed to fill the lakes again.

Ursula and her father, of course, could see the valley bloom, a dense and vivid forest as rich as the Amazon's.

'You see the trees, Ursula, the same ones your father saw?'

'All of them, and millions of flowers, too. Nevada's a wonderful garden now. Our eyes are filling the whole state with blossom. One flower makes the desert bloom.'

'And one tree becomes a forest, one drop of water a whole lake. Time took that away from us, Ursula, though for a brief while the first men and women probably saw the world as a paradise. When did you learn to see?'

'When I brought Dad out here, after they shut the clinic.

But it started during our drive. Later we went back to the mirrors. They helped me open my eyes. Dad's already were open.'

'The solar mirrors — I should have gone back myself.'

'Slade waited for you, doctor. He waited for months. He's almost out of time now — I think he only has enough time for one more flight.' Ursula dusted the sand from the sheet. For all the Amazon blaze during their fugues, clouds of dust blew into the apartment, a gritty reminder of a different world. She listened to the silent wind. 'Never mind, doctor, there are so many doors. For us it was the mirrors, for you it was that strange camera and your wife's body in sex.'

She fell silent, staring at the verandah with eyes from which time had suddenly drained. Her hand was open, letting the sand run away, fingers outstretched like a child's to catch the brilliant air. Smiling at everything around her, she tried to talk to Franklin, but the sounds came out like a baby's burble.

Franklin held her cold hands, happy to be with her during the fugue. He liked to listen to her murmuring talk. So-called articulate speech was an artefact of time. But the babbling infant, and this young woman, spoke with the lucidity of the timeless, that same lucidity that others tried to achieve in delirium and brain-damage. The babbling new-born were telling their mothers of that realm of wonder from which they had just been expelled. He urged Ursula on, eager to understand her. Soon they would go into the light together, into that last fugue which would free them from the world of appearances.

He waited for the hands to multiply on his watch-dial, the sure sign of the next fugue. In the real world beyond the clock, serial time gave way to simultaneity. Like a camera with its shutter left open indefinitely, the eye perceived a moving object as a series of separate images. Ursula's walking figure as she searched for Franklin had left a hundred replicas of herself behind her, seeded the air with a host of identical twins. Seen from the speeding car, the few frayed palm trees along the road had multiplied themselves across the screen of Trippett's mind, the same forest of palms that Franklin had perceived as he moved across the desert. The lakes had been the multiplied images of the water in that tepid motel pool, and the blue streams were the engine coolant running from the radiator of his overturned car.

During the following days, when he left his bed and began to move around the apartment, Franklin happily embraced the fugues. Each day he shed another two or three minutes. Within only a few weeks, time would cease to exist. Now, however, he was awake during the fugues, able to explore this empty suburb of the radiant city. He had been freed by the ambiguous dream that had sustained him for so long, the vision of his wife with Slade, then copulating with the surrounding hills, in this ultimate infidelity with the mineral kingdom and with time and space themselves.

In the mornings he watched Ursula bathe in the piazza below his verandah. As she strolled around the fountain, drying herself under a dozen suns, Soleri II seemed filled with beautiful, naked women bathing themselves in a city of waterfalls, a seraglio beyond all the fantasies of Franklin's childhood.

At noon, during a few last minutes of time, Franklin stared at himself in the wardrobe mirror. He felt embarrassed by the continued presence of his body, by the sticklike arms and legs, a collection of bones discarded at the foot of the clock. As the fugue began he raised his arms and filled the room with replicas of himself, a procession of winged men each dressed in his coronation armour. Free from time, the light had become richer, gilding his skin with layer upon layer of golden leaf. Confident now, he knew that death was merely a failure of time, and that if he died this would be in a small and unimportant way. Long before they died, he and Ursula would become the people of the sun.

It was the last day of past time, and the first of the day of forever.

Franklin woke in the white room to feel Ursula slapping his shoulders. The exhausted girl lay across his chest, sobbing into her fists. She held his wristwatch in her hand, and pressed it against his forehead.

'...wake, doctor. Come back just once...'

'Ursula, you're cutting –'

'Doctor!' Relieved to see him awake, she rubbed her tears into his forehead. 'It's Dad, doctor.'

'The old man? What is it? Has he died?'

'No, he won't die.' She shook her head, and then pointed to the empty terrace across the piazza. 'Slade's been here. He's taken Dad!'

She swayed against the mirror as Franklin dressed. He searched unsteadily for a hat to shield himself from the sun, listening to the rackety engine of Slade's microlight. It was parked on the service road near the solar farm, and the reflected light from its propeller filled the air with knives. Since his arrival at Soleri he had seen nothing of Slade, and hoped that he had flown away, taking Marion with him. Now the noise and violence of the engine were tearing apart the new world he had constructed so carefully. Within only a few more hours he and Ursula would escape from time for ever.

Franklin leaned against the rim of the washbasin, no longer recognizing the monk-like figure who stared at him from the shaving mirror. Already he felt exhausted by the effort of coping with this small segment of conscious time, an adult forced to play a child's frantic game. During the past three weeks time had been running out at an ever faster rate. All that was left was a single brief period of a few minutes each day, useful only for the task of feeding himself and the girl. Ursula had lost interest in cooking for them, and devoted herself to drifting through the arcades and sundecks of the city, deep in her fugues.

Aware that they would both perish unless he mastered the fugues, Franklin steered himself into the kitchen. In the warm afternoons the steam from the soup tureen soon turned the solar city into an island of clouds. Gradually, though, he was teaching Ursula to eat, to talk and respond to him even during the fugues. There was a new language to learn, sentences whose nouns and verbs were separated by days, syllables whose vowels were marked by the phases of the sun and moon. This was a language outside time, whose grammar was shaped by the contours of Ursula's breasts in his hands, by the geometry of the apartment. The angle between two walls became an Homeric myth. He and Ursula lisped at each other, lovers talking between the transits of the moon, in the language of birds, wolves and whales. From the start, their sex together had taken away all Franklin's fears. Ursula's ample figure at last proved itself in the fugues. Nature had prepared her for a world without time, and he lay between her breasts like Trippett sleeping in his meadows.

Now he was back in a realm of harsh light and rigid perspectives, wristwatch in hand, its mark on his forehead.

'Ursula, try not to follow me.' At the city gates he steadied her against the portico, trying to rub a few more seconds of time into her cooling hands. If they both went out into the desert, they would soon perish in the heat of that angry and lonely sun. Like all things, the sun needed its companions, needed time leached away from it...

As Franklin set off across the desert the microlight's engine began to race at full bore, choked itself and stuttered to a stop. Slade stepped from the cockpit, uninterested in Franklin's approach. He was still naked, except for his

114

goggles, and his white skin was covered with weals and sunsores, as if time itself were an infective plague from which he now intended to escape. He swung the propeller, shouting at the flooded engine. Strapped into the passenger seat of the aircraft was a grey-haired old man, a scarecrow stuffed inside an oversize flying jacket. Clearly missing the vivid flash of the propeller, Trippett moved his hands up and down, a juggler palming pieces of light in the air.

'Slade! Leave the old man!'

Franklin ran forward into the sun. His next fugue would begin in a few minutes, leaving him exposed to the dreamlike violence of Slade's propeller. He fell to his knees against the nearest of the mirrors as the engine clattered into life.

Satisfied, Slade stepped back from the propeller, smiling at the old astronaut. Trippett swayed in his seat, eager for the flight to begin. Slade patted his head, and then surveyed the surrounding landscape. His gaunt face seemed calm for the first time, as if he now accepted the logic of the air and the light, the vibrating propeller and the happy old man in his passenger seat. Watching him, Franklin knew that Slade was delaying his flight until the last moment, so that he would take off into his own fugue. As they soared towards the sun, he and the old astronaut would make their way into space again, on their forever journey to the stars.

'Slade, we want the old man here! You don't need him now!'

Slade frowned at Franklin's shout, this hoarse voice from the empty mirrors. Turning from the cockpit, he brushed his sunburnt shoulder against the starboard wing. He winced, and dropped the chromium pistol on to the sand.

Before he could retrieve it, Franklin stood up and ran through the lines of mirrors. High above, he could see the reflection of himself in the collector dish, a stumbling cripple who had pirated the sky. Even Trippett had noticed him, and rollicked in his seat, urging on this lunatic aerialist. He reached the last of the mirrors, straddled the metal plate and walked towards Slade, brushing the dust from his trousers.

'Doctor, you're too late.' Slade shook his head, impatient with Franklin's derelict appearance. 'A whole life too late. We're taking off now.'

'Leave Trippett...' Franklin tried to speak, but the words slurred on his tongue. 'I'll take his place...'

'I don't think so, doctor. Besides, Marion is out there somewhere.' He gestured to the desert. 'I left her on the runways for you.'

Franklin swayed against the brightening air. Trippett was still conducting the propeller, impatient to join the sky. Shadows doubled themselves from Slade's heels. Franklin pressed the wound on his forehead, forcing himself to remain in time long enough to reach the aircraft. But the fugue was already beginning, the light glazed everything around him. Slade was a naked angel pinioned against the stained glass of the air.

'Doctor? I could save...' Slade beckoned to him, his arm forming a winged replica of itself. As he moved towards Franklin his body began to disassemble. Isolated eyes watched Franklin, mouths grimaced in the vivid light. The silver pistols multiplied.

Like dragonflies, they hovered in the air around Franklin long after the aircraft had taken off into the sky.

The sky was filled with winged men. Franklin stood among the mirrors, as the aircraft multiplied in the air and crowded the sky with endless armadas. Ursula was coming for him, she and her sisters walking across the desert from the gates of the solar city. Franklin waited for her to fetch him, glad that she had learned to feed herself. He knew that he would soon have to leave her and Soleri II, and set off in search of his wife. Happy now to be free of time, he embraced the great fugue. All the light in the universe had

116

come here to greet him, an immense congregation of particles.

Franklin revelled in the light, as he would do when he returned to the clinic. After the long journey on foot across the desert, he at last reached the empty air base. In the evenings he sat on the roof above the runways, and remembered his drive with the old astronaut. There he rested, learning the language of the birds, waiting for his wife to emerge from the runways and bring him news from the sun.

Theatre of War

Author's preface

After three hundred years, could civil war again divide the United Kingdom? Given rising unemployment and industrial stagnation, an ever more entrenched class system and a weak monarchy detaching itself from all but its ceremonial roles, is it possible to visualize the huge antagonisms between the extreme left and right resolving themselves in open civil conflict? I take it for granted that despite its unhappy experience in South East Asia the intervention of the United States to defend its military and economic investments would be even more certain than it was in Viet Nam. I also assume that the television coverage would be uninterrupted and all-pervasive, and have therefore cast it in the form of a TV documentary, of the type made popular by World in Action.

Part One
LONDON UNDER SIEGE

STREET BATTLE

Inner London, a back street in Lambeth, where confused street-fighting is taking place. Tank engine noise forms a continuous background to heavy machine-gun fire and intercom chatter. Twenty soldiers, five American and the rest British, move from door to door, firing at the other end of the street, where Big Ben is visible above the shabby roof-tops. Helicopter gunships circle overhead. A tank stops by a house and soldiers dart in. A moment later a woman emerges, followed by three exhausted children and an old man carrying his bedroll. They run past with stunned faces. Bodies lie everywhere. Two negro GIs drag away a dead enemy soldier with shoulder-length hair. Stitched to his camouflage jacket is a Union Jack. The picture freezes, and the camera zooms in on the Union Jack until it fills the screen, soaked in the soldier's blood.

WORLD IN ACTION TITLES
Superimposed over the bloody Union Jack: 'Civil War'

Commentator
One street battle is over, but the civil war goes on. After four years no solution is in sight. American casualties total 30,000 dead, a hundred thousand missing and wounded. A million British civilians have died. Despite mounting criticism at home America pours more and more troops into what is now the European Viet Nam. But the fighting continues. This week the Liberation Front launched a major offensive against a dozen cities. Here in Lambeth a suicide squad fights its way to within 800 yards of the House of Parliament. How long can the British government survive? Will peace ever come? *World in Action* is here to find out.

STREET BATTLE
The fighting is over, and the government forces are mopping up. They flush frightened civilians from the basements and herd them away past the bodies of enemy soldiers. At the junction with the main road in the background a British Airways advertisement hoarding is riddled with bullet holes. A sullen-faced young English woman is frisked roughly by British troops while others tear the Union Jacks from dead enemy soldiers. The tank drags away a tangle of bodies lashed together by their wrists. In a jeep loaded with

119

looted cameras, radios and record players pop music blares from the intercom.

CUT TO NIGHT-TIME SOHO

Background of garish lights, pin-table arcades, strip clubs. GIs spill out of cars and move into a bar.

Commentator
GIs relax during a weekend of R & R. Two days ago they were fighting off a Liberation Front offensive in the suburbs of Manchester. As the United Nations talks of settlement and both sides in the civil war plan new offensives, what do the ordinary GIs think of the prospects for peace?

1st US soldier (reclining in bar)
It's a very ticklish situation over here. It's hard to analyse and get a complete grasp of the whole story, because from my position at least you can't get a glimpse of the whole subject. You know, you don't know what motivates these people. Peace seems to be very far off, at least to me it does.

Commentator
Tell me, do you think it's all worth it?

2nd US soldier
It's hard to say. I think we're just, as I see it, we're fooling around. That's about all. I do think we should be here.

Commentator
What's the alternative to fooling around?

3rd US soldier
Well, they call it a civil war. If it's a war, it should be that. They push us, we push them, it's a kind of stalemate as I see it right now. I think we should show them who's boss. Because what I've seen of the gooks over here, they're going to fight, *fight* – you know? – and just keep on fighting.

2nd US soldier

If you're fighting a war, fight it like a war, with all the mass of power we have. Power in reserve, air power, land power, and power from the sea. We've got battleships offshore can pound this place to absolutely nothing.

Commentator

Tough talk from the GIs as they relax, but in the bright light of day, as London picks up the pieces after the latest NLF offensive, what exactly is the present military position? Can either side win this war? In New York today President Reagan was asked what kind of settlement he would hope to resolve. The President replied: 'I don't think we can talk about settlement of the war at this point. I think we *can* talk about our willingness to accept a coalition or fusion government. At least it could very well be talked about in the open before we begin to talk about negotiations.' President Reagan spent the day in New York City where he addressed a luncheon audience and denied that the war is indefensible, a view strongly challenged by Congressional leaders of both parties. But how accurate is the picture which the American public at large has of the civil war?

NEWSREEL

Medley of clips – Civilians running as GIs and British government troops move across a tenement courtyard, firing at a roof-top sniper; helicopters circling a fortified Wembley Stadium; street execution near Piccadilly Circus of three NLF soldiers in plain clothes, hands wired, as a crowd outside a sandbagged cinema looks on; corpses of children laid out in a village hall; gun-battle outside a Top-Rank Bingo hall; crowd at Bellevue, Manchester, fun-fair backing off a roundabout to reveal a body pumped up and down by a wooden unicorn to the Wurlitzer music; lines of strip clubs in Oxford, entrances guarded by Military Police barring civilians; pound-notes over-printed 'One Dollar'; tanks

121

ringing Parliament Square; shops loaded with consumer goods; a huge bonfire of Union Jacks; elderly refugees camping on the canted decks of a multi-storey car-park in Dover, guarded by uncertain-looking GIs straight off a troop-carrier; government troops demolishing a rebel earth bunker lined with carefully framed portraits of George VI during World War II, visiting munitions factories and bombed-out East Enders.

Commentator
As each day passes, life in the government-held areas becomes less and less tolerable. London is a city under siege. Manchester, Liverpool and Birmingham are the last remaining strongholds of government support, defended by massive American forces. The countryside belongs to the NLF. The continuous infiltration of the London suburbs by guerilla battalions mingling with the local population has brought the front line to everyone's doorstep. Bomb outrages, kidnappings, street battles with snipers, the assassination of local political leaders – these are part of day to day life. In the five years of its exile in Riyadh, uneasy guests of the Saudi royal house, the monarchy has lost all credibility, unwilling to commit its waning prestige to either side in the civil war. Meanwhile, in the London over which the Queen once reigned, the black market flourishes. Millions of dollars worth of American goods pour into the capital, propping up a juke-box economy of pirate TV networks, thousands of bars and brothels. In many towns and suburbs the main unit of currency is the illegal NLF pound sterling. The government-backed British dollar is despised. Anything can be bought, but nothing has any value. More and more young people slip away to join the Liberation Front. Doctors, engineers, trained mechanics desert to the enemy forces. They leave behind a population that consists mainly of the old middle class and an army of bartenders, croupiers and call-girls. London is now a gigantic Las Vegas, the

largest light-bulb in the world, ready to blow out in a hail of rebel machine-gun fire.

COMMENTATOR IN GROSVENOR SQUARE
American Embassy in background, surrounded by tanks. GIs and British troops patrol. Muted gunfire near distance, but civilians go about their ordinary lives without concern.

Commentator
As both sides mount major offensives, I'm standing in Grosvenor Square, the old Eisenhowerplatz of World War II, once again the headquarters of the American and British government forces. This time they are fighting, not the superbly equipped German Wehrmacht with its panzer divisions, but a British peasant army. None the less, can the government forces and their American allies win? Will the war ever end?

INTERVIEW WITH BRITISH SUPREME COMMANDER
A sometime heir to the English throne, the 36-year-old commander of the government forces is an aggressive, media-wise opportunist with pearl-handled revolver, black flying suit and white silk scarf. He is shown parading in a succession of military uniforms, firing a sub-machine-gun at a rifle range, inspecting a dispirited platoon of government troops, boarding his roof-top helicopter which he flies himself to inspect the attacks breaking out all over the city (though the viewer is unsure whether he is about to make a discreet bunk), and generally trying to boost the morale of his entourage. His line is confident but embittered; he knows he has lost his throne by his involvement with the puppet regime. He hates the NLF, but the Americans more. His hero is Rommel, but his style is James Bond.

British Commander
As Commander of the British loyalist forces my job is to win

the war and unify the country again. The enemy is increasingly fighting out of desperation. Our intelligence tells us that he is running out of men, out of steam and out of material. He simply doesn't have the economic potential to maintain a war. The people in Europe and the United States who criticize the war don't really know what's going on. Quite evidently the people of this country don't want anything to do with the people up north, or with the communist way of life.

Commentator
You don't feel, General, that you and the Americans are forcing a form of government on the people of this country?

British Commander
No, we're not forcing anything on them. The United States feels that this is a good place to stop communist aggression, and if the government forces do win, and I know they will, we'll have, firstly, a good ally, and we'll have stopped communist aggression from taking over the United Kingdom and eventually France and everywhere else.

(Points to map showing blacked-out areas of British Isles.)

Our forces are now moving forwards into a series of major confrontations with the other side, so I think you can look forward to when that map will be white again. Then I know the Americans will be glad to leave for home.

COMMENTATOR BACK IN GROSVENOR SQUARE
Maps in hand, he addresses camera.

Commentator
Meanwhile, however, the British Commander is reported to be asking the US President for yet more troops. How many soldiers will be needed to hold the line against the NLF? Despite the General's easy optimism it isn't his map which most people look at, but this one issued by the NLF.

124

(Lifts other map. Black areas encircle major cities, all the countryside.)

It's this one they consult if they want to visit their relatives in the country or move to another town. It's this one they use if they want to defect to the NLF.

EXPLOSION BURSTS ACROSS SQUARE

Camera wobbles, swings wildly. Panic, people running. Commentator ducks, then starts talking in confused way.

Commentator

... there's been a – it looks, it looks as if a sniper. What seems to be happening is that a –

CROWD FORMING A ROUGH CIRCLE AROUND A JEEP

GIs push people back, and look down at the body of an American officer in the front seat, blood pouring from wound. Pop music blares from the intercom radio a few inches from his face.

Radio Announcer

We have a list of the latest curfew regulations. In the inner capital the curfew bell is midnight to 6 am for Kensington, Knightsbridge and Battersea and from 10 to 7 am for the 3rd Air Cav. and support units in –

GI REACHES OVER AND SWITCHES OFF RADIO

Commentator

Five minutes ago a senior American officer was assassinated as he sat in his jeep outside the American officers' club here in Grosvenor Square. An NLF killer in civilian clothes stepped through the lunch-time crowd and fired a single shot, then disappeared back into the crowd. The officer, Colonel Wilson J. Tucker, a military adviser in the 'hearts and minds' mission, widely suspected of being a cover for a

125

CIA murder squad, died within a few seconds. All that's known about the killer is that he was 'young', probably in his early twenties, a safe enough assumption at a time when most of the young men and women here have long since left to join the Liberation Front, at a time when to be young automatically invites the attentions of the military police and the hostility of the old and middle-aged who provide the last support for the puppet regime. As one visiting Canadian journalist put it to me...

CANADIAN JOURNALIST IN HOTEL BAR

Canadian Journalist
All the NLF have to do to win this war is wait ten years. By then everyone on the government side will be either dead or in a wheelchair.

SHOTS OF YOUNG PEOPLE AT CAMP SITE
Police hustling them about. Older people watching as girls and young men have their hair shaved.

Commentator
Certainly one of the most striking divisions in British life is the now unbridgeable gulf between the young and the old. Even if the peace talks start and a settlement is finally reached will it be possible for them to live together in one society? A legacy of resentment, intolerance and sexual jealousy has been fed by years of violence and open war. At a time when the twin pillars of life in the government areas are the strip club and the US dollar, does Britain any longer possess the political and social institutions to make possible a real society?

Canadian journalist
I don't see Parliament now as a functioning entity in any way. It's a rump of older Members of Parliament and extreme right-wingers, a blow-hole for all kinds of unpleasant

126

fascist gas. As a legislature it's non-existent. Let's face the facts, the British government is a puppet regime, *and it means to keep it that way*. The economy has a real balance of payments surplus for the first time in thirty years, thanks to American war-spending and the GI dollar. Baby, nobody on this side says 'Yank, go home'. They're more likely to offer you their sister – or their mother. Their sister's on the other side.

Commentator
Patriotism takes many forms. Is it significant, though, that the flag of the Liberation Front is the Union Jack, long-standing symbol of the union of Britain's major provincial areas – a symbol now hated and feared by the government supporters? To what extent can the government itself provide any prospects for unity?

INTERVIEW WITH BRITISH PRIME MINISTER

A former Labour Prime Minister recalled to office, to lead the all-party coalition, he sits uneasily inside a sandbagged Downing Street, literally ducking every time a shot is heard. He is surrounded by armed guards, but looks shifty and dispirited. All too clearly he is at the Americans' mercy, and has no ideas for bringing the war to an end.

Commentator
Could I ask you first, Prime Minister, are you hopeful at the moment at the outlook for peace?

Prime Minister
Well, it depends very much on what the other side wants to do. The latest offensives – attacks against the ordinary people of this country – don't suggest that they're particularly sincere in their talk about wanting a settlement.

Commentator
Do you envisage that the departure of the American troops will create problems? If one travels around London one sees

127

that a large part of the local economy is geared to serving the GI. When the GI is gone, won't there be problems for those people who presently are...

Prime Minister

Well, this contains the same problem shared by all those countries which have had large American forces on their soil – Germany, Japan, Viet Nam. I think it will be a good thing because we shall be back to normal and a lot of people will have to look for a living within their means. They'll have to give up a lot of windfall benefits which come from the war and create social problems. We've now got in this country a class of people created by the war, and I think it's a good thing that this will stop.

Commentator

Childhood for most of the children in London has been a strange life with the American dollar, hasn't it? The American dollar has been the way they passed their childhood. When that in the form of the GI goes, are they not going to have a lot of problems?

Prime Minister

I'm sure they will. They'll be economic problems mainly. I think we're all going to have to find ourselves, so to speak, a painful process whether it's an individual or a nation. I think there's going to be a period of readjustment, possibly of turbulence, but they must go through the process. Perhaps if they'd gone through it twenty years ago there wouldn't be a war now.

GENERAL VIEWS OF PEOPLE HANGING AROUND ENTRANCES TO AMERICAN BASES

Commentator

Can the British people find themselves? Can they go through the painful process of re-establishing themselves as a single nation? With 70 per cent of the economy tied to the

128

war, with the revenues from North Sea oil long since sold off to the Germans and Japanese, will ordinary people be able to make the adjustments necessary to living with the other side? In short, do they want the war to end at all? *World in Action* visited a village in the front line to see how the bulk of the population is facing up to the reality of the war.

GENERAL PICTURE OF SMALL TOWN IN BUCKINGHAMSHIRE

Barbed wire, road blocks, troops and armoured cars. Gunfire in the distance.

Commentator

Here at Cookham, only twenty miles or so from the centre of London, the 'windfall benefits' of the war are more likely to be a sniper's bullet or a barrage of enemy mortar shells. This is one of the so-called pacified villages. By day the British and American forces occupy the bunkers and pillboxes. In the evening they withdraw with the local administrators to a fortified enclave near the American base at Windsor. At night the Liberation Front moves in. At this moment their advance positions are no more than two hundred yards away, their sentries watching us through binoculars. None of these villagers will talk to us. All are assumed to be Liberation Front sympathizers, but in fact they are professional neutrals, living on the edge of a giant razor that could cut them down at any moment. They farm the fields, work in the garages and shops, and wait for the Americans to leave. Strangest of all here, there is no one between the ages of four and forty.

TANK APPEARS, FOLLOWED BY BRITISH AND AMERICAN SOLDIERS

Commentator

A special task force arrives, part of a self-styled Pacification

129

Probe that will advance ten miles into country recently occupied by the Liberation Front. One tank, ten GIs of the First Cavalry Division, and thirty British soldiers are under the command of Captain Arjay Robinson. *World in Action* is going with them to see what happens.

CAPTAIN ROBINSON BRIEFING HIS UNIT IN THE VILLAGE HALL
The GIs, heavily armed with flak jackets and radio-equipped helmets, sit at the front, the British troops with two elderly officers at the back.

Captain Robinson
The primary mission of Alpha Company is to conduct a reconnaissance and pacification. Circles indicate supply caches within the area, also known parking areas, primarily wheeled vehicles and larger trucks. There are also some small yellow dots, these indicate known positions where we have seen tanks. There are tanks in the area definitely. As I see it right now we're going to have two companies controlling the fire base. We'll play it real loose, play it by ear pretty much as to where we're going and the times that we'll go. We're going down there and kill the enemy where we find him and come back.

Part Two
PACIFICATION PROBE

Commentator
A Pacification Probe prepares to set off. It's 6.35 am, and the thirty British soldiers who will do the major part of the fighting – and the major part of the dying – wait quietly in the background as the American tank crew and radio spe-

130

cialists prepare their equipment. The American weapons and communications are now so sophisticated that the British troops can barely understand them. Many of these men will defect on this mission, many more will die. What are they up against? Last month a Swedish film crew smuggled itself through the front lines. Their brief film shows what life is like within the Liberation Front.

NEWSREEL OF LIBERATION FRONT AREAS
Mountains, tunnel entrances guarded by young soldiers and armed young women. Union Jacks flying. People working in factories. Alternative technology, windmills, small-scale smelting works, machine shops, hand-looms. Children everywhere, thin but healthy. Kibbutz atmosphere, young mothers in khaki mini-skirts with babies and rifles. Slit trenches, men with rifles move through fields around burnt-out American tank. Callisthenics in drill-hall, communal singing around flag. Indoctrination sessions, 18-year-old political commissar addressing doctors and nursing staff in hospital. Children taking part in people's theatre, 4-year-olds dressed in parody US military uniforms miming bombing attacks on sturdy villagers. Everywhere slogans, loudspeakers, portraits of George VI.

Swedish voice-over
The mountains of Scotland and Wales are the main strongholds of the National Liberation Front. In the four-year war against the British central government hundreds of underground schools and factories have been built. From here supplies and equipment go out to the front line. By now all the agricultural areas of England are under control of the Liberation Front. The soldiers and peasants are organized in communes, the women farming and looking after the children while the men are fighting. Their leaders are young. There are few old people here. Everywhere morale is high, they are confident that they have won the war and that the

Americans must soon leave. They are Scottish, Welsh, people from the northern and western provinces of England, West Indians, Asians and Africans. For four years they have been bombed but they are still fighting.

COOKHAM
Cut to Captain Robinson on the turret of his tank.

He scans the empty fields. Nothing moves. In the compound below the soldiers have finished readying their weapons and equipment. The *World in Action* commentator puts on US combat clothing, strapping a gun around his waist, trying out heavy boots. A helicopter clatters overhead.

AFN radio announcer
…in the southern outskirts of London last night a guerilla unit fired a 107 mm rocket, killing one civilian and wounding four others. First Air Cav. ground elements in Operation Pegasus killed 207 enemy in scattered contacts yesterday, with friendly casualties light. First Division Marines killed 124 in two separate battles in Northern Province. The leathernecks ambushed enemy elements, calling in support by artillery and air attack. The marines took no casualties while killing 156 communists…

Commentator
Half an hour from now the forty men of Alpha Company will set out from Cookham. As we move off across this guerilla-infested countryside two companies of combat engineers will have flown in to the target area by helicopter. They will deal with any local opposition. The main function of Alpha Company, this so-called pacification probe, is to re-establish the government's authority. The thirty British soldiers and the District Administrator will stay on after the Americans have left, recruiting local militia, setting up a fortified hamlet and redirecting the area's agriculture. The target area is at a key point on the M4 Motorway to the

132

south-west. To keep this road open the government forces are setting up a chain of fortified villages along its 200-mile length.

CAPTAIN ROBINSON CHECKING HIS MEN'S EQUIPMENT

Commentator
Alpha Company's commander, Captain Arjay Robinson, is already a veteran of this war. Thirty-two years old, he comes from Denver, Colorado, and is a graduate of West Point. He is married to a clergyman's daughter and has three children, none of whom he has seen in the two years he has been here. A career soldier, he has already decided to stay here until the Americans leave.

SERGEANT PALEY CHECKING TANK TREADS

Commentator
His second-in-command is Sergeant Carl W. Paley, a 26-year-old bachelor from Stockton, California, where he was general manager of a local radio station owned by his father. Like Captain Robinson, he has had almost no contact with the ordinary people of this country. To him they form a grey background of blurred faces – girls he meets in the bars outside the base camps, old men who clean out the barracks or serve as waiters in the sergeants' mess. Apart from the prostitutes, the only young English people he will see are likely to be in the sights of his guns. Last month Alpha Company was involved in a major action in which over 250 enemy soldiers were killed, a third of them women auxiliaries. But to Sergeant Paley they are merely 'Charley' – a blanket term carried over from Viet Nam, or 'the gooks'.

TANK ENGINE STARTS UP
American soldiers climb aboard, the British form up into a column behind it.

Commentator
As for the British troops who will go with them — like all
the Americans here, Sergeant Paley holds them in little more
than contempt. Underfed and ill-equipped, the British
troops have to provide their own food and bedding. During
the next six hours the Americans will ride to the battlefield
on their tank. The thirty British will walk. Mostly men in
their forties, with a few younger men drafted from the penal
battalions, they represent the residue of the armies conscripted by the government three years ago, armies now
decimated by casualties and desertions.

MAJOR CLEAVER
A thick-set man with British army moustache climbs on to
the tank beside Captain Robinson. He wears American
boots, fawn trousers, brown leather jacket and carries US
Army revolver.

Commentator
The only Britisher to whom the Americans pay any attention
is Major Cleaver, the District Administrator who will be in
charge of the pacified village. A former regular army officer,
Major Cleaver is one of several thousand DAs sent out by the
British government to run the civil administration of the
recaptured areas. Part political commissar, part judge and
jury, Major Cleaver will literally have the power of life and
death over the people living under his rule, a power that he
and his fellow DAs have been quick to exercise in the past.

THE CONVOY MOVES OFF
The infantry spread out ahead and to the side of the tank.
They follow a road through wooded terrain with meadows
and abandoned farms on either side. Now and then there is
a halt as the tank is brought up.

Captain Robinson
Helicopters are the thing that's happening these days. You

can get in there real fast with heavy suppressive fire, and if you need to be pulled out you can get out real fast.

Sergeant Paley
It's definitely the way to fight a ground war.

Captain Robinson
As I see it now we're going to have two companies controlling the fire base, Bravo and Charley, who will go in by helicopter. They'll clear the landing zone by the time we get in there, so the tactical side of the operation should be finalized. It's also better from the psychological aspect that we don't get involved on the tactical side too much.

Commentator
You mean the actual fighting around the village?

Captain Robinson
That's correct.

RADIO OPERATOR PASSES MESSAGE TO CAPTAIN ROBINSON
Tank halts.

Commentator
But for Bravo and Charley Companies, who are supposed to be going in by helicopter, today is not the day for fighting a war. The weather in the target area has closed in, and the helicopters have returned to base. Alpha Company gets ready to move on alone, every man here hoping that the weather will clear.

Sergeant Paley
This country, weather's the main thing. It rains a lot and you're very wet most of the time, but you know as a soldier you can't ask for a certain territory to fight on because you just have to make the best of what terrain you have.

135

Commentator
Sergeant, what do you think of the chances of peace here?

Sergeant Paley
Well, I think they're ... I don't know, as I see it as long as Charley's got a weapon and some ammo and using it he's not going to give up. I think he's pretty much got his heart in it, giving his own people a hard time here.

Commentator
How do you feel it's all going?

Sergeant Paley
Well, it's going well for the Cavs, I know that. Wherever we go we run into Charley – I know he doesn't last very long.

Commentator
Tell me, sergeant, why are you in England?

Sergeant Paley
Why am I in England? Well, curiosity, I guess. I just wanted to know what the war was like.

Commentator
What is the war like?

Sergeant Paley
Well, it's all right, I guess. For a year I'd say it's a good experience. You really learn a lot from it.

Major Cleaver
Naturally one hopes that peace will come to the country as soon as possible. Positions have become very entrenched during the past year, there's a legacy of bitterness on both sides. This is not the kind of civil war that resolves anything.

Commentator
What about the fighting itself? Don't you find it difficult to be shooting at your own people?

Major Cleaver

They're not our own people any longer. This is the whole point of the war. They're the enemy now, and peace isn't going to turn them overnight into our friends.

Commentator

But aren't there a lot of desertions from the army?

Major Cleaver

Not as many as there used to be. Most of the men realize that conditions here are a lot better than they are on the other side. The bombing has killed hundreds of thousands of people. Sitting here eating C rations is a lot more comfortable than being boiled alive in napalm.

THE COLUMN MOVES ON

Slow penetration of forest on either side of the road. We see the tank stuck in a small stream. Cameo shots of individual American and British soldiers. Fade to early afternoon.

A long shot of farmland and the motorway on the left, the village to the right. Nothing moves. The camera turns and we see the American and British troops dug in along the edge of the field facing the village. It has been raining but the sky has cleared. Everything is very quiet. Machine-guns and weapons being set up. The tank is hidden in trees. Captain Robinson scans the low sky through binoculars.

Commentator

Three o'clock the same afternoon. Alpha Company has arrived at its objective. No signs of the helicopters, so Captain Robinson and his men will have to go in alone. How many Liberation Front soldiers are facing us? Perhaps fifty, perhaps a hundred. Will they fight? Or will they fade away into the surrounding countryside, leaving their women and children behind until night comes again?

THE AMERICANS AND BRITISH ARE WATCHING QUIETLY

A farmer appears and walks along a pathway on the far side of the field. He carries a rifle over his shoulder. Sergeant Paley watches him cross the sights of his machine-gun. Nobody moves.

THE VILLAGE IS COMING TO LIFE AFTER THE RAIN-STORM

Young men and women appear. They go about their work. A stall is set up and food is distributed. Young mothers in their khaki mini-skirts drop their children into the communal crèche. Others move towards the fields and farm buildings with rifles over their shoulders. A damp Union Jack is run up on the village flag-pole. Meanwhile, the American and British government forces watch quietly over their gun-sights. Through the zoom lens we focus on individual soldiers, and then on individual villagers in their sights: a young man with a headband who is the kibbutz leader; his girlfriend with a baby; a coloured girl with a pistol on her waist. The leader speaks through a megaphone, the sounds just carrying across the field. He is making some kind of joke, and everyone in the village laughs.

THE FIRST FARMERS WALK OUT ACROSS THE FIELD

They are still unaware of the government forces, and carry their rifles slung casually over their shoulders. One of them, a young Pakistani, has spotted something moving across the field. He follows it between the cabbages, then bends down and picks it up. It is an American cigarette pack. Puzzled, he looks up. Ten feet away he sees the barrel of a light machine-gun aimed at him by Sergeant Paley. Crushing the pack in his hand, he opens his mouth to shout.

CAPTAIN ROBINSON SIGNALS

Sergeant Paley opens fire straight at the young Pakistani. Torn apart, he falls among the cabbages. Massive firing breaks out. The other young men and women in the field are shot down. Mortar fire is directed at the village, the tank lumbers forward, its heavy gun opening fire. Through the long-distance lens we see isolated men and women being shot down, others running for shelter. The food stall is overturned. A barn is burning. Captain Robinson signals again, and the men move forward in a general advance, firing as they go. The *World in Action* commentator and Major Cleaver move up with them, taking shelter behind the tank. Counter fire is coming from the village, from a small blockhouse built behind a bicycle shed. Two British soldiers are shot down. In the village now everything is burning. Bodies lie around, there are burning motorcycles and food scattered everywhere.

EVERYTHING IS QUIET

The battle has been over an hour or so. A few fires are still burning, smoke drifting towards the distant motorway. The British government troops break down the doors of the houses. They stare at the lines of bodies, mostly young women and children. Six prisoners have their hands wired together. The remaining villagers are driven out into the field.

2nd Commentator

Two hours ago, in the attack on this small village beside the M4, the *World in Action* commentator was killed. As he followed the first wave of American soldiers he was shot by an unknown enemy sniper and within a few minutes died of his wounds. His report on this war has been shown as he made it.

VILLAGERS SQUATTING IN FIELD

GIs prepare demolition charges.

139

2nd Commentator
Alpha Company prepares to pull out. The weather has closed in again, and there will be no support coming in by helicopter. The action is called off at the request of Major Cleaver. Ten British soldiers have been killed or wounded. Without the Americans and their tank he could never hold the village.

Captain Robinson
We're moving them out, just generally get them out of the way. You can bomb their houses flat easier that way without the conscience of the people on your mind. Put them out in the field.

EXPLOSIONS RIP APART VILLAGE BUILDINGS
Close-up of bodies of rebel soldiers dragged along in mud behind the tank. The column pulls out through the dusk, heading back to Cookham.

Major Cleaver
To help another human being out, it's worth the expense and loss of life. It's just that I sometimes wonder whether some of the people that I know who have died knew what they were dying for. That's about the hardest thing to think of, you know. If a man doesn't know why he's dying, it's a bad way to go.

Acknowledgment: For all the dialogue above, to General Westmoreland, President Thieu of South Viet Nam, Marshall Ky and various journalists, US and ARVN military personnel.

The Dead Time

Without warning, as if trying to confuse us, the Japanese guarding our camp had vanished. I stood by the open gates of the camp with a group of fellow-internees, staring in an almost mesmerized way at the deserted road and at the untended canals and paddy-fields that stretched on all sides to the horizon. The guard-house had been abandoned. The two Japanese sentries who usually waved me away whenever I tried to sell them cigarettes had given up their posts and fled with the remainder of the military police to their barracks in Shanghai. The tyre-prints of their vehicles were still clearly visible in the dust between the gate-posts.

Perhaps even this hint at the presence of Japanese who had imprisoned us for three years was enough to deter us from crossing the line into the silent world outside the camp. We stood together in the gateway, trying to straighten our shabby clothing and listening to the children playing in the compound. Behind the nearest of the dormitory blocks several women were hanging out their morning's washing, as if fully content to begin another day's life in the camp. Yet everything was over!

Although the youngest of the group – I was then only twenty – on an impulse I casually stepped forward and walked into the centre of the road. The others watched me as I turned to face the camp. Clearly they half-expected a shot to ring out from somewhere. One of them, a consultant engineer who had known my parents before the war separated us, raised his hand as if to beckon me to safety.

The faint drone of an American aircraft crossed the empty bank of the river half a mile away. It flew steadily towards us, no more than a hundred feet above the paddy-fields, the young pilot sitting forward over his controls as he peered down at us. Then he rolled his wings in a gesture of greeting and altered course for Shanghai.

Their confidence restored, the others were suddenly around me, laughing and shouting as they set off down the road. Six hundred yards away was a Chinese village, partly hidden by the eroded humps of the burial mounds built on the earth causeways that separated the paddies. Already substantial supplies of rice beer had been brought back to the camp. For all our caution, we were not the first of the internees to leave the camp. A week earlier, immediately after the news of the Japanese capitulation, a party of merchant seamen had climbed through the fence behind their block and walked the eight miles to Shanghai. There they had been picked up by the Japanese gendarmerie, held for two days and returned to the camp in a badly beaten state. So far all the others who had reached Shanghai — whether, like myself, searching for relations, or trying to check up on their businesses — had met with the same fate.

As we strode towards the village, now and then looking back at the curious perspectives of the camp receding behind us, I watched the paddies and canals on either side of the road. In spite of everything I had heard on the radio broadcasts, I was still not certain that the war was over. During the past year we had listened more or less openly to the various radios smuggled into the camp, and had followed the progress of the American forces across the Pacific. We had heard detailed accounts of the atom-bomb attacks — Nagasaki was little more than 500 miles from us — and of the Emperor's call for capitulation immediately after. But at our camp, eight miles to the east of Shanghai at

142

the mouth of the Yangtse, little had changed. Large numbers of American aircraft crossed the sky unopposed, no longer taking part in any offensive action, but we soon noticed that none had landed at the military airfield adjacent to our camp. Dwindling but still substantial numbers of Japanese troops held the landscape, patrolling the airfield perimeter, the railway lines and roads to Shanghai. Military police continued to guard the camp, as if guaranteeing our imprisonment through whatever peace might follow, and kept little more than their usual distance from the two thousand internees. Paradoxically, the one positive sign was that since the Emperor's broadcast no food had arrived for us.

Hunger, in fact, was my chief reason for leaving the camp. In the confusion after Pearl Harbor I had been separated from my parents by the Japanese occupation authorities and imprisoned in a stockade in the centre of Shanghai reserved for male allied nationals. Eighteen months later, when the American bombing began, the stockade was closed and the prisoners scattered at random among the cluster of large camps for families with children in the countryside surrounding Shanghai. My parents and young sister had spent the war in another of these some twenty miles to the west of the city. Although their condition was probably as bad as my own I was convinced that once I reached them everything would be well.

'It looks as if they're gone. They must have cleared out with everything overnight.'

At the entrance to the village the man next to me, a garage owner from Shanghai, pointed to the abandoned houses. Catching our breath after the brisk walk, we gazed down at the empty alleys and shuttered windows. Not a Chinese was in sight, though only the previous afternoon they had been doing a profitable trade with groups of internees from the camp, bartering rice beer for watches, shoes and fountain pens.

143

While the others conferred, I wandered away to the ruins of a ceramics factory on the outskirts of the village. Perhaps under the impression that its kilns were some sort of military installation, the Americans had bombed the factory again and again. A few of the buildings were still standing, but the courtyards were covered with thousands of pieces of broken crockery. Uncannily, these seemed to have been sorted out into various categories of table-ware. I walked across a carpet of porcelain soup spoons, all too aware of the fact that the only noise in this entire landscape was coming from my feet.

For the villagers to have left so suddenly, after all their struggles through the war, could only mean that they were frightened of something they were sure would take place in their immediate locality. During the past year they had attached themselves to our camp, selling a few eggs through the barbed wire and later, when they themselves began to be hungry, trying to break through the fences in order to steal the tomatoes and root-crops which the internees grew on every square foot of vacant soil. At one time we had recruited the Japanese guards to help us strengthen the wire to keep out these pilferers. In the last months the circle of starving or ailing older villagers planted outside the camp gates – none were ever admitted, let alone fed – grew larger every day.

Yet for some reason they had all gone. As I walked back from the factory perimeter my companions were discussing the best route across the paddy-fields to Shanghai. They had ransacked several of the houses and were now sitting on the piles of broken crockery with bottles of rice beer. I remembered the rumours we had heard that before they surrendered the Japanese planned to slaughter their civilian prisoners.

I looked back along the road to the camp, aware of its curious confusion of vulnerability and security. The water-tower and three-storey concrete blocks seemed to rise from the lines of burial mounds. The camp had been a Chinese middle school. We had arrived after dark, and I had never seen it from the outside before, just as I had never physically entered the empty landscape surrounding the camp which had been an intimate part of my life all these years.

I listened to my companions' increasingly random discussion. Apart from the consultant engineer and the garage owner, there were two Australian seamen and a hotel barman. Already I was certain that they had no idea of the hazards facing them, and that as long as I remained with them I would never reach my parents. Their one intention was to get drunk in as many as possible of the dozens of villages between here and Shanghai.

Five minutes after I left them, however, as I walked back along the road to the camp, I heard the sounds of a Japanese military truck coming behind me from the village. Armed soldiers of the gendarmerie leaned on the cabin above the driver, guarding my five former companions who sat on the floor on either side of the tail-gate. Their faces had an ashen and toneless look, like those of men woken abruptly from sleep. Alone of them, an Australian seaman glanced up from his bound wrists and stared at me, as if failing to recognize who I was.

I continued to walk towards the camp, but the truck stopped in front of me. None of the soldiers spoke or even beckoned me to climb aboard, and already I knew that we were not being given a lift back to the camp.

Without thinking, I had a sudden presentiment of death, not of my own but of everyone else around me.

For the next three days we were held in the gendarmerie barracks attached to the military airfield, where some hundred or so allied aircrew shot down during the air attacks on Shanghai had been concentrated in an attempt to dissuade the American bombers from strafing the hangars and runways. To my relief, we were not mistreated. The Japanese sat around listlessly, no longer interested in us and gazing up in a melancholy way at the American aircraft which endlessly crossed the sky. Already supplies were being parachuted into our camp. From the window of our cell we could see the coloured canopies falling past the water-tower.

Clearly the war was over, and when a gendarmerie sergeant released us from the cell and ordered us into the barracks square I took for granted that we were about to be turned loose at the airfield gates. Instead, we were put aboard the same truck that had brought us here and driven under guard to the nearby railway station that served as a military depot on the Shanghai-Nanking line.

The first to jump down from the truck, I looked around at the ruined station buildings, well aware that the last train had stopped here some two months beforehand. Apart from the aircraft overhead, the landscape remained as deserted as it had been on the day of our abortive escape. On all sides was the debris of war – rusting trucks, a paddy-field used as a dump for worn-out tyres, a line of tank ditches half-filled with water that ran towards a small football stadium set back from the road, a blockhouse covered with leaking sandbags built at the entrance to the station. But the Chinese had gone, vacating the landscape as if at last deciding to leave us to our own resources, to whatever pointless end we cared to make.

'It looks as if we're going to play soccer,' one of the Australian seamen called back to the others as he and I followed the three guards towards the stadium.

'Some stunt for the Red Cross,' someone else commented. 'Afterwards, make sure they take us back to the camp.'

But already I could see into the stadium, and had realized that whatever else took place, we would not be playing football. We climbed the concrete entrance tunnel into the ground, a circle of yellowing grass in the centre of which two trucks were parked. Sections of the empty stand had

146

been used by the Japanese as a warehouse, and several soldiers patrolled the seats high above us, guarding what seemed to be a pile of looted furniture. A party of smartly uniformed military stood by the two trucks, waiting for us to approach. At their head was a young Eurasian interpreter in a white shirt.

As we walked towards them we looked down at the ground at our feet. Stretched out on the frayed grass were some fifty corpses, laid out in neat rows as if arranged with great care and devotion. All were fully dressed and lay with their feet towards us, arms at their sides, and I could see from the bright pallor of their faces that these people, whoever they were, had only recently died. I paused by a young nun wearing a full habit and wimple whose broad mouth had only just begun to take on its death grimace. Around her, like the members of her flock, were three children, heads to one side as if they had fallen asleep before death.

Watched by the Japanese soldiers and the young interpreter, and by the sentries guarding the furniture in the stands, we walked slowly past the corpses. Apart from two middle-aged Chinese, a man and a woman lying next to each other who might have been husband and wife, all were European and American, and from the worn state of their shoes and clothing seemed to be internees like ourselves. I passed a large ruddy-haired man in brown shorts with a gun-shot wound in his chest, and an elderly woman in a print dress who had been shot in the jaw, but at first sight none of the other bodies revealed any signs of violence.

Twenty feet ahead of me one of the Japanese soldiers by the trucks had moved his rifle. Behind me my companions stepped back involuntarily. The garage owner stumbled against me, for a moment holding my shoulder. I listened to the sound of an American aircraft overhead, the noise of its engine magnified by the concrete bowl of the stadium. It seemed insane that we would be shot here ten days after the war had ended in full view of our rescuers, but already I was convinced that we would not die. Yet again I had that same presentiment of death I had inexplicably felt before our arrest.

One of the Japanese officers, wearing full uniform under a short rain-cape, spoke briefly. I noticed that he was standing beside a small card-table on which rested two wicker baskets containing bottles of saki and parcels of boiled rice wrapped in leaves. For some bizarre reason I assumed that he was about to give me a prize.

The Eurasian in the white shirt came up to me. His face had the same passivity of the Japanese. No doubt he realized that once the Kuomintang forces arrived his own life would be over, like those of the fifty people lying on the stadium grass.

'You're all right?' he asked me. After a pause, he nodded at the Japanese officer. Then, almost as an afterthought, he said, 'You can drive a truck?'

'Yes...' The presence of the armed Japanese made any other answer pointless. In fact I had not driven any vehicle since the outbreak of war, and before that only my father's Plymouth car.

'Of course we can.' The garage owner had pulled himself together and joined us. He looked back at our four companions, who were now separated from us by the tract of corpses. 'We can both drive, I'm an experienced mechanic. Who are all those people? What happened to them?'

'We need two drivers,' the interpreter said. 'You know the Protestant cemetery at Soochow?'

'No, but we can find it.'

'That's good. It's only sixty miles, four hours, then you can go free. You take these people to the Protestant cemetery.'

'All right.' The garage owner had again held my shoulder, this time to prevent me changing my mind, though I already had no intention of doing so. 'But who are they all?'

The interpreter seemed to have lost interest. Already the Japanese soldiers were lowering the tail-gates of the trucks. 'Various things,' he said, patting his white shirt. 'Some illnesses, the American planes...'

An hour later we had loaded the fifty corpses on to the two trucks and after a trial circuit of the stadium had set off in the direction of Soochow.

Looking back on those first few hours of freedom as we drove together across the empty landscape fifteen miles to the south-east of Shanghai, I am struck by the extent to which we had already forgotten the passengers whose destination had made that freedom possible. Of course neither Hodson, the garage owner, nor myself had the slightest intention of driving to Soochow. As I could see from his manner as the six of us loaded the last of the corpses on to his truck, his one ambition was to turn right on the first road to Shanghai and abandon the truck and its contents in a side street – or, conceivably, given a sudden access of humanity, outside the Swiss embassy. In fact, my chief fear was that Hodson might leave me to be picked up by a Japanese patrol before I had mastered the truck's heavy steering and gear-box.

Luckily we had all been so exhausted by the effort of loading the bodies that the Japanese had not noticed my fumbling efforts to start and control the truck, and within half an hour I was able to keep a steady fifty yards behind Hodson. Both vehicles were plastered with military stickers pasted to the windshields and fenders, presumably assuring our passage through whatever Japanese units we might meet. Twice we passed a platoon sitting with its packs and rifles on the railway line, waiting for a train that would never come, but otherwise the landscape was deserted, not a single Chinese visible. Circumspectly, though, Hodson followed the route to Soochow marked on the road-map given to us by the Eurasian interpreter.

For myself, I was content to make this circuit of Shanghai, as I had no wish to drive the truck with its cargo of corpses through the centre of the city on my way to my parents' camp. Once I had cleared the western suburbs of the city I would turn north off the Soochow road, hand the vehicle over to the first allied command post — our new-found freedom had convinced me that the war would finally be over by the afternoon — and complete the short journey to my parents' camp on foot.

The prospect of seeing them, after all these years, within literally a few hours made me feel light-headed. During the three days in the gendarmerie barracks we had been given almost nothing to eat, and I now picked at the boiled rice in the wicker basket on the seat beside me. Even the sight of the corpses whose feet and faces were shaking loose beneath the tarpaulin of Hodson's truck did nothing to spoil my appetite. As I had lifted the bodies on to the two trucks I had immediately noticed how well-fleshed most of them were, far better fed than any of us had been in our camp. Presumably they had been imprisoned in some special internment centre, and had unluckily fallen foul of the American air-attacks.

At the same time the absence, with few exceptions, of any wounds or violence suggested one or two unsettling alternatives — plague, perhaps, or some sudden epidemic. Steering the truck with one hand and eating my rice with the other, I eased my foot off the heavy accelerator, opening the interval slightly between Hodson and myself. But for all this I was hardly concerned about the bodies. Too many people had already died in and around our camp. The business of loading the corpses into the trucks had placed a certain mental distance between them and myself. Handling all those bodies, pulling on the stiffening arms and legs, pushing their buttocks and shoulders over the tail-gates, had been like an extended wrestling match with a party of strangers, a kind of forced intimacy that absolved me from all future contact or obligation.

An hour after leaving the stadium, when we had covered some ten miles, Hodson began to slow down, his truck bumping over the rutted road surface at little more than walking pace. Some half a mile from the river, we had entered a landscape flooded by a slack, brown water. Untended canals and drowned paddies stretched away on all sides, and the road had become little more than a series of narrow causeways. The vanished peasants had built their burial mounds into the shoulders of the road, and the ends of the cheap coffins protruded like drawers from the rain-washed earth, lockers ransacked by the passing war. Across the paddies I could see a boom of scuttled freighters that blocked the river, funnels and bridge-houses emerging from the swollen tide. We passed another abandoned village, and then the green shell of a reconnaissance aircraft shot down by the Americans.

Ten feet in front of me, Hodson's truck bumped along the roadway, the heads of his corpses nodding vigorously like sleepers assenting in some shared dream. Then Hodson stopped and jumped down from his cabin.

He laid the map across the bonnet of my truck, then pointed along the broad canal we had been following for the past ten minutes. 'We've got to cross this before we reach the main road. Somewhere up ahead there's a sluice-bridge. It looks too small to have been bombed.'

With his strong hands he began to tear away the stickers pasted to the fenders and windshield of my truck. Though gaunt and undernourished, he looked strong and aggressive. The experience of driving a vehicle again had clearly restored his confidence. I could see that he had been helping himself liberally to his bottle of saki.

He bent down under the tail-gate of his truck and felt the left inside tyre. I had noticed the vehicle tilting when we first reached the canal.

'Going soft – no damn spares either.' He stood up and gazed into the rear of the truck, and with a single sweep of

151

one arm flung back the tarpaulin, like a customs official exposing a suspicious cargo. Nodding to himself, he stared at the bodies piled across each other.

'Right, we rest here and finish the food, then find this bridge. First, let's make things easier for ourselves.'

Before I could speak he had reached into the truck and seized one of the corpses by the shoulders. He jerked it away from its companions and hurled it head-first into the canal. That of a freckle-skinned man in his early thirties, it surfaced within a few seconds in the brown water and slowly drifted away past the reeds.

'Right, we'll have the nun next.' As he hauled her out he shouted over his shoulder, 'You get on with yours. Leave a few behind just in case.'

Ten minutes later, as we sat with our bottles of saki on the bank of the canal, some twenty of the corpses were in the water, moving slowly away from us in the sluggish current. Pulling them down had almost exhausted me, but the first sips of the saki bolted through my bloodstream, almost as intoxicating as the boiled rice I had eaten. The brusque way in which we had ridden ourselves of our passengers no longer unsettled me – though, curiously, as I stood by the tail-gate pulling the bodies on to the ground I had found myself making some kind of selection. I had kept back the three children and a middle-aged woman who might have been their mother, and thrown into the water the Chinese couple and the elderly woman with the jaw-wound. However, all this meant nothing. What mattered was to reach my parents. It was clear to me that the Japanese had not been serious about our delivering the bodies to the Protestant cemetery at Soochow – the two nuns exposed this as no more than a ruse, relieving them of some local embarrassment before the Americans landed at the airfield.

Hodson was asleep beside his truck. His saki bottle followed the corpses down the canal. After throwing a few stones at it, I passed the next hour watching the vapour trails of the American aircraft and thinking with increasing optimism about the future, and about seeing my parents and sister later that afternoon. We would move back to our house in the French concession. My father would re-open his brokerage business, and no doubt train me as his assistant. After years of war and privation, Shanghai would be a boom city again ... everything would once again return to normal.

This pleasant reverie sustained me, when Hodson had woken blearily and clambered back into his cabin, as we set off in our lightened trucks. I was beginning to feel hungry again, and regretted eating all my rice, particularly as Hodson had thrown his into the canal. But then I heard Hodson shout something back to me. He was pointing to the sluice-bridge a hundred yards in front of us.

When we reached it we found that we were not the only ones hoping to make the crossing.

Parked on the approaches to the bridge, its light machine-gun unguarded, was a camouflaged Japanese patrol car. As we stopped, the three-man crew had climbed on to the bridge and were trying to close the gates which would carry us across. Seeing us arrive, the sergeant in charge walked over to us, scanning the few stickers which Hodson had not torn from our trucks. We stepped down from the cabins, waiting as the sergeant inspected our cargos without comment. He spoke a few words in Japanese to Hodson, and beckoned us over to the bridge.

As we looked down at the sluices, we could see immediately what had blocked the bridges and prevented the gates from closing. Humped together against the vents were well over a dozen of the corpses which Hodson and I had pitched into the canal an hour earlier. They lay together like mattresses, arms and legs across each other, some face down, others staring at the sky.

To my shock I realized that I recognized each of them. That presentiment of death — though not my own nor of

153

these drowned creatures – which I had felt so often during the past days returned to me, and I looked round at Hodson and the three Japanese as if expecting them immediately to fulfil this unconscious need.

'Well, what do they want?' Hodson was arguing aggressively with the Japanese sergeant, who for some reason was shouting at me in a suddenly high-pitched voice. Perhaps he realized that I might respond to his instructions for reasons of my own. I looked at his face and angular shoulders, wrists that were little more than sticks, well aware that he was as hungry as myself.

'I think they want us to get them out,' I said to Hodson. 'Otherwise, we can't get across. They know we threw them into the water.'

'For God's sake…' Exasperated, Hodson pushed past the Japanese and clambered down the bank of the canal. Waist-deep among the corpses, he began to sort them out with his strong arms. 'Aren't they going to help?' he called up in an aggrieved way when the Japanese made no effort to move.

Needless to say, Hodson and I were obliged to lift the bodies out ourselves. They lay on the bank like a party of exhausted bathers, in a strange way almost refreshed by their journey down the canal. The blood had been washed from the jaw-wound of the elderly woman, and I could see for the first time the image of a distinct personality. The sunlight lit the line of moist faces, illuminating the exposed hands and ankles.

'Well, we can get across now.' Looking down at his drenched trousers as the Japanese closed the sluice-gates, Hodson said to me 'Let's get on with it. We'll leave them here.'

I was staring at the face of the elderly woman, visualizing her talking to me, perhaps about her childhood in England or her long missionary years in Tientsin. Beside her the washed robes of the young nun had an almost spectral

154

blackness, which gave her white hands and face an extraordinary glow. I was about to join Hodson when I noticed that the Japanese were also gazing at the bodies. All I could see was their intense hunger, as if they were eager to become my passengers.

'I think we should put them back on the trucks,' I said to Hodson. Fortunately, before he could remonstrate with me the sergeant had come over to us, beckoning us to work with his pistol.

Hodson helped me to load the first ten bodies on to the back of my truck. Then, unable to contain his anger any more, he seized the bottle of saki from the cabin, pushed past the Japanese and climbed into his truck. Shouting something at me, he drove on to the bridge and set off along the opposite bank of the canal.

For the next half hour I continued to load my vehicle, pausing to rest for a few minutes after I had carefully stowed each of the bodies. The effort of dragging them up the bank and lifting them into the truck almost exhausted me, and when I had finished I sat numbly for ten minutes behind my steering wheel. As I started the engine and drove on to the bridge with my heavy cargo the Japanese watched me without comment.

Fortunately, my anger at Hodson soon revived me. I clenched the wheel tightly in both hands, forehead touching the windshield, as the overladen vehicle lumbered down the uneven canal road. To have taken my saki mattered nothing, but to leave me with more than my fair share of corpses, without a map in this water-logged maze ... Within half a mile of leaving the Japanese I was tempted to stop and heave a dozen of the bodies – I had the clearest picture in my mind of those who were Hodson's rather than my own – back into the water. Only the nun and the elderly woman I would allow on board. But I knew that once I stopped I would lose all hope of catching up with Hodson.

Ahead of me, above the fields of uncropped sugar-cane, I could see the poles and straggling telegraphy wire that marked one of the main roads to Shanghai. I pressed on towards it, the vehicle rolling from side to side on the earth track. Behind me the bodies were sliding about as if in some huge scrimmage, their heads banging the sides of the truck. It was now a short period after noon, and a potent but not altogether unpleasant stench had filled the cabin. In spite of its obvious source, it seemed in some way to be refracted and amplified by the odours of my own body, almost as if my hunger and exhaustion were acting as the catalyst for the process of putrefaction. A plague of flies had descended on the truck, and covered the outer surface of the rear window behind my head, so that I was unable to see if the Japanese were following me in their scout car. I could still see the profound sense of loss in their eyes as they had watched me leave, and I almost regretted that I had not taken them with me. Far from my being their prisoner, it was they who in some way belonged to the bodies lying behind me.

Before I could reach the main Shanghai road the radiator of the engine had boiled, and I wasted a full half an hour waiting for it to cool. In order to lighten the load on the engine, I decided to throw off Hodson's corpses. There was now no chance whatever of catching up with him, and he was almost certainly speeding through the suburbs of Shanghai for a first look at his garage. Somehow I would find my own way to my parents' camp.

I climbed on to the back of the truck, and clambered among the bodies piled together. Gazing down at the yellowing faces between my feet, I realized that I recognized almost all of them – the nuns and the Chinese couple, the elderly woman and the three children, a slim young man of my own age with an amputated left hand, a pregnant woman in her early twenties who vaguely resembled my sister. These belonged to my flock, whereas Hodson's intruders were as distinct and separate as the members of a rival clan. Their leader was clearly a small, elderly man with a bare-chested body like a grey monkey's, whose sharp eyes had seemed to follow me all day as I lifted him on and off the trucks.

I bent down to seize him by the shoulders, but for some reason my hands were unable to touch him. Once again I felt that presentiment of death I had sensed so many times, surrounding me on all sides, in the canal beside the road, in the fields of sugar-cane and the distant telegraph wires, even in the drone of an American aircraft crossing far overhead. Only I and the passengers aboard this truck were immune.

I tried to pick up another of the corpses, but again my hands froze, and again I felt the same presentiment, an enclosing wall that enveloped us like the wire fence around our camp. I watched the flies swarm across my hands and over the faces of the bodies between my feet, relieved now that I would never again be forced to distinguish between us. I hurled the tarpaulin into the canal, so that the air could play over their faces as we sped along. When the engine of the truck had cooled I refilled the radiator with water from the canal, and set off towards the west.

It was without surprise, an hour later, that I came across Hodson's truck, and was able to make up the full complement of my passengers.

Where Hodson himself had gone I never discovered. Five miles down the Shanghai road, after two further delays to rest the engine, I found the truck abandoned by a Japanese road-block. In the afternoon haze the surface of the road seemed to be speckled with gold, nodes of bright light reflected from hundreds of spent cartridge cases. The Japanese here had fought a vigorous engagement, perhaps with some intruding patrol of Kuomintang troops. Webbing and empty ammunition boxes lay in the tank ditch dug across the road. Unable to drive around this obstacle, Hodson had presumably set off on foot.

I stopped beside his abandoned truck, listening to the harsh beat of my engine in the deserted air. A hundred yards behind me a narrow lane led across a field of sugar-cane in a westerly direction, and with luck would carry me a little further on my circuit of Shanghai.

First, however, I had to take on my additional passengers. At the time, as I carried the dozen corpses from Hodson's truck and lifted them on to my own, it occurred to me more than once to give up the entire enterprise and set off on foot myself after Hodson. But as we turned off the road and rolled down the lane between the fields of sugar-cane I felt a curious kind of comfort that we were all together, almost a sense of security at the presence of my 'family'. At the same time the urge to rid myself of them still remained, and given the opportunity – a lift, perhaps, in a passing Kuomintang vehicle – I would have left them at the first chance. But within this empty landscape they did at least provide an element of security, particularly if a hostile Japanese patrol came across me. Also, for the first time I had begun to feel a sense of loyalty towards them, and the feeling that they, the dead, were more living than the living who had deserted me.

The afternoon sun had begun to set. I woke in the cabin of the truck to find that I had fallen asleep beside a broad canal whose brown surface had turned almost carmine in the fading light. In front of me were the approaches to an empty village, the single-storey dwellings concealed by the dark fronds of the wild sugar-cane. All afternoon I had been lost in a golden world, following the sun as it moved away from me across the drowned paddies and silent villages. I was certain that I had covered some twenty miles – the apartment houses of the French concession were no longer visible along the horizon.

158

My last attempt to free myself from the corpses took place that night. At dusk I stepped from the cabin of the truck and walked through the sugar-cane, breaking the stems and sucking the sweet pith. From the back of the truck the corpses watched me like a hostile chorus, their inclined heads slyly confiding in each other. I too at first resented this nourishment flowing through me, meagre though it was. As I revived, however, leaning against the radiator grille of the truck, I was suddenly tempted to release the handbrake and roll the vehicle forward into the blood-stained canal. As a result of committing myself to this lunatic troupe of passengers, ferrying them from the football stadium to some destination they had never agreed upon, I had lost the chance of seeing my parents that day.

Under the cover of darkness – for I would not have dared to commit this act by daylight – I returned to the truck and began to remove the bodies one by one, throwing them down on to the road. Clouds of flies festered around me, as if trying to warn me of the insanity of what I was doing. Exhausted I pulled the bodies down like damp sacks, ruthlessly avoiding the faces of the nuns and the children, the young amputee and the elderly woman.

At this point, when I had nearly destroyed everything I had been allowed by circumstances to achieve, I was saved by the arrival of a party of bandits. Armed American merchant seamen, renegade Kuomintang and quisling auxiliaries of the Japanese, they arrived by sampans and rapidly occupied the village. Too tired to run from them, I crouched behind the truck, watching these heavily armed men move towards me. For some reason, although I knew they would kill me, I had no sense whatever of that presentiment of death.

At the last moment, when they were only twenty feet away, I lay down in the darkness among the circle of corpses, taking my position between the young nun and the elderly woman. The ferocious flight of the thousand flies came to a stop, and I could hear the heavy step of the bandits and the sounds of their weapons. Lying there in the darkness in the circle of the dead, I watched them halt and peer into the truck, arms raised across their mouths. Unable to approach us, they waited for a few minutes and then returned to the village. All night, as they roamed from house to house, kicking down the doors and breaking the furniture, I lay in the circle of corpses. Towards dawn two of the Kuomintang soldiers came and began to search the pockets of the dead. Staring at the sky, I listened to them panting beside me, and felt their hands on my thighs and buttocks.

At dawn, when they left in their motorized sampans, the flies returned. I stood up and watched the sun rising through the dark forests of sugar-cane. Waiting for its disc to touch me, I summoned my companions to their feet.

From this time onwards, during the confused days of my journey to my parents' camp, I was completely identified with my companions. I no longer attempted to escape them. As we drove together through that landscape of war and its aftermath, past the endless canals and deserted villages, I was uncertain whether the events taking place spanned a few hours or many weeks. I was almost sure that by now the war should have been over, but the countryside remained empty, disturbed only by the sounds of the American aircraft overhead.

For much of the time I followed the westerly course of the river, a distant presence which provided my only compass bearing. I drove carefully along the broken roads that divided the paddy-fields, anxious not to disturb my passengers lying together behind me. It was they who had saved me from the bandits. I knew that in a sense I was their representative, the instrument of the new order which I had been delegated by them to bring to the world. I knew that I now had to teach the living that my companions were not merely the dead, but the last of the dead, and that soon the whole planet would share in the new life which they had earned for us.

One small example of this understanding was that I no longer wished for food. I looked out from the cabin of the truck at the wide fields of sugar-cane beside the river, knowing that their harvest would no longer be needed, and that the land could be turned over to the demands of my companions.

One afternoon, after a brief thunderstorm had driven the American aircraft from the sky, I reached the bank of the river. At some time a battle had been fought here among the wharfs and quays of a small Japanese naval air base. In the village behind the base there were shallow wells filled with rifles, and a pagoda housing a still intact anti-aircraft gun. All the villagers had fled, but to my amazement I found that I was not alone.

Seated side by side in a rickshaw that had been abandoned in the central square of the village were an elderly Chinese and a child of ten or so whom I took to be his grand-daughter. At first glance they looked as if they had hired the rickshaw a few hours beforehand and ridden out here to view this small battlefield that I too was now visiting. I stopped my truck, stepped down from the cabin and walked over to them, looking around to see if their coolie was present.

As I approached, the child climbed from the rickshaw and stood passively beside it. I could see now that, far from being a spectator, her grandfather had been seriously wounded in the battle. A large piece of shrapnel had driven through the side of the rickshaw into his hip.

In Chinese I said to him, 'I'm making my way to the Soochow road. If you wish, you and your grand-daughter are welcome to ride with my companions.'

He made no reply, but I knew from his eyes that despite his injuries he had immediately recognized me, and under-

161

stood that I was the harbinger of all that lay before him. For the first time I realized why I had seen so few Chinese during the past days. They had not gone away forever, but were waiting for my return. I alone could repopulate their land.

Together the child and I walked down to the concrete ramp of the naval air base. In the deep water below the wharf lay the drowned forms of hundreds of cars rounded up from the allied nationals in Shanghai and dumped here by the Japanese. They rested on the river bed twenty feet below the surface, the elements of a past world that would never be able to reconstitute itself now that I and my companions, this child and her grandfather had taken possession of the land.

Two days later we at last reached the approaches to my parents' camp. During our journey the child sat beside me in the cabin of the truck, while her grandfather rode comfortably with my companions. Although she complained of hunger to begin with, I patiently taught her that food was no longer necessary to us. Fortunately I was able to distract her by pointing out the different marks of American aircraft that crossed the sky.

After we reached the Soochow road the landscape was to change. Close to the Yangtse we had entered an area of old battlegrounds. On all sides the Chinese had emerged from their hiding places and were waiting for my arrival. They lay in the fields around their houses, legs stirring in the water that seeped across the paddy-fields. They watched from the embankments of the tank-ditches, from their burial mounds and from the doors of their ruined houses.

Beside me the child slept fitfully on the seat. Free of any fear of embarrassing her, I stopped the truck and took off my ragged clothes, leaving only a crude bandage on my arm that covered a small wound. Naked, I knelt in front of the vehicle, raising my arms to my congregation in the fields

162

around me, like a king assuming his crown at his coronation. Although still a virgin, I exposed my loins to the Chinese watching me as they lay quietly in the fields. With those loins I would seed the dead.

Every fifty yards, as I approached the distant water-tower of my parents' camp, I stopped the truck and knelt naked in front of its boiling radiator. There was no sign of movement from the camp compound, and I was sure now what I would find there.

The child lay motionlessly in my arms. As I knelt with her in the centre of the road, wondering if it were time for her to join my companions, I noticed that her lips still moved. Without thinking, giving way to what then seemed a meaningless impulse, I tore a small shred of flesh from the wound on my arm and pressed it between her lips.

Feeding her in this way, I walked with her towards the camp a few hundred yards away. The child stirred in my arms. Looking down I saw that her eyes had partly opened. Although unable to see me, she seemed aware of the movement of my stride.

From the gates of the camp, on the roofs of the dormitory blocks, on the causeways of the paddy-fields beyong the wire, people were moving. Their figures were coming towards me, advancing waist-deep through the stunted sugarcane. Astonished, I pressed the child to my chest, aware of her mouthing my flesh. Standing naked a hundred yards from the truck, I counted a dozen, a score, then fifty of the internees, some with children behind them.

At last, through this child and my body, the dead were coming to life, rising from their fields and doorways and coming to greet me. I saw my mother and father at the gates of the camp, and knew that I had given my death to them and so brought them into this world. Unharmed they had passed into the commonwealth of the living, and of the other living beyond the dead.

I knew now that the war was over.

The Smile

Now that a nightmare logic has run its course, it is hard to believe that my friends and I thought it the most innocent caprice when I first brought Serena Cockayne to live with me in my Chelsea house. Two subjects have always fascinated me – woman and the bizarre – and Serena combined them both, though not in any crude or perverse sense. During the extended dinner parties that carried us through our first summer together three years ago her presence beside me, beautiful, silent and forever reassuring in its strange way, was surrounded by all kinds of complex and charming ironies.

No one who met Serena failed to be delighted by her. She would sit demurely in her gilt chair by the sitting-room door, the blue folds of her brocade gown embracing her like a gentle and devoted sea. At dinner, when my guests had taken their seats, they would watch with amused and tolerant affection as I carried Serena to her place at the opposite end of the table. Her faint smile, the most delicate bloom of that peerless skin, presided over our elaborate evenings with unvarying calm. When the last of my guests had gone, paying their respects to Serena as she watched them from the hall, head inclined to one side in that characteristic pose of hers, I would carry her happily to my bedroom.

Of course Serena never took part in any of our conversations, and no doubt this was a vital element of her appeal. My friends and I belonged to that generation of men who

164

had been forced in early middle age, by sexual necessity if nothing else, to a weary acceptance of militant feminism, and there was something about Serena's passive beauty, her immaculate but old-fashioned make-up, and above all her unbroken silence that spelled out a deep and pleasing deference to our wounded masculinity. In all senses, Serena was the kind of woman that men invent.

But this was before I realized the true nature of Serena's character, and the more ambiguous role she was to play in my life, from which I wait now with so much longing to be freed.

Appropriately enough — though the irony then escaped me completely — I first saw Serena Cockayne at the World's End, in that area at the lower end of the King's Road now occupied by a cluster of high-rise apartment blocks but which only three years ago was still an enclave of second-rate antique shops, scruffy boutiques and nineteenth-century terrace housing over-ripe for redevelopment. Pausing on my way home from the office by a small curio shop announcing its closing-down sale, I peered through the sulphur-stained windows at the few remnants on display. Almost everything had gone, except for a clutch of ragged Victorian umbrellas collapsed in the corner like a decaying witch and an ancient set of stuffed elephant's feet. These dozen or so dusty monoliths had a special poignancy, all that remained of some solitary herd slaughtered for its ivory a century earlier. I visualized them displayed secretly around my sitting-room, filling the air with their invisible but dignified presences.

Inside the shop a young woman attendant sat behind a marquetry desk, watching me with her head tilted to one side as if calculating in a patient way how serious a customer I might be. This unprofessional pose, and her total lack of response as I entered the shop, ought to have warned me off, but already I had been struck by the young woman's unusual appearance.

What I first noticed, transforming the dingy interior of the shop, was the magnificence of her brocaded gown, far beyond the means of a sales girl at this dowdy end of the King's Road. Against a lustrous blue field, a cerulean of almost Pacific deepness, the gold and silver patterning rose from the floor at her feet, so rich that I almost expected the gown to surge up and engulf her. By comparison, her demure head and shoulders, white bust discreetly revealed by the low bodice, emerged with an extraordinary serenity from this resplendent sea, like those of a tamed and domestic Aphrodite seated calmly astride Poseidon. Although barely beyond her teens, her hair had been dressed in a deliberately unfashionable style, as if lovingly assembled by an elderly devotee of twenties' film magazines. Within this blonde helmet her features had been rouged and powdered with the same lavish care, eyebrows plucked and hairline raised, without any sense of pastiche or mock nostalgia, perhaps by an eccentric mother still dreaming of Valentino.

Her small hands rested on her lap, apparently clasped together but in fact separated by a narrow interval, a stylized pose that suggested she was trying to hold to her some moment of time that might otherwise slip away. On her mouth hung a faint smile, at once pensive and reassuring, as if she had resigned herself in the most adult way to the vanishing world of this moribund curio shop.

'I'm sorry to see you're closing down,' I remarked to her. 'That set of elephant's feet in the window...there's something rather touching about them.'

She made no reply. Her hands remained clasped their millimetres apart, and her eyes stared in their trance-like way at the door I had closed behind me. She was sitting on a peculiarly designed chair, a three-legged contraption of varnished teak that was part stand and part artist's easel.

Realizing that it was some sort of surgical device and that

she was probably a cripple – hence the elaborate make-up and frozen posture – I bent down to speak to her again.

Then I saw the brass plaque fastened to the apex of the teak tripod on which she sat.

SERENA COCKAYNE

Attached to the plaque was a dusty price ticket. '£250'.

In retrospect, it is curious that it took me so long to realize that I was looking, not at a real young woman, but at an elaborate manikin, a masterpiece of the doll-maker's art produced by a remarkable virtuoso. This at last made sense of her Edwardian gown and antique wig, the twenties' cosmetics and facial expression. None the less, the resemblance to a real woman was uncanny. The slightly bowed contours of the shoulders, the too-pearly and unblemished skin, the few strands of hair at the nape of the neck that had escaped the wig-maker's attentions, the uncanny delicacy with which the nostrils, ears and lips had been modelled – almost by an act of sexual love – together these represented a *tour de force* so breath-taking that it all but concealed the subtle wit of the whole enterprise. Already I was thinking of the impact this life-size replica of themselves would have on the wives of my friends when I first introduced them to it.

A curtain behind me was drawn back. The owner of the shop, an adroit young homosexual, came forward with a white cat in his arms, chin raised at the sound of my delighted laughter. Already I had taken out my cheque-book and had scribbled my signature with a flourish befitting the occasion.

So I carried Serena Cockayne to a taxi and brought her home to live with me. Looking back at that first summer we spent together I remember it as a time of perpetual good humour, in which almost every aspect of my life was en-

167

riched by Serena's presence. Decorous and unobtrusive, she touched everything around me with the most delicious ironies. Sitting quietly by the fireplace in my study as I read, presiding like the mistress of the house over the dining-table, her placid smile and serene gaze illuminated the air.

Not one of my friends failed to be taken in by the illusion, and all complimented me on bringing off such a coup. Their wives, of course, regarded Serena with suspicion, and clearly considered her to be part of some adolescent or sexist prank. However, I kept a straight face, and within a few months her presence in my house was taken for granted by all of us.

Indeed, by the autumn she was so much a part of my life that I often failed to notice her at all. Soon after her arrival I had discarded the heavy teak stand and substituted a small gilt chair on which I could carry her comfortably from room to room. Serena was remarkably light. Her inventor – this unknown genius of the doll-maker's art – had clearly inserted a substantial armature, for her posture, like her expression, never changed. Nowhere was there any indication of her date or place of manufacture, but from the scuffed patent-leather shoes that sometimes protruded below the brocade gown I guessed that she had been assembled some twenty years earlier, possibly as an actress's double during the great days of the post-war film industry. By the time I returned to the shop to inquire about her previous owners the entire World's End had been reduced to rubble.

One Sunday evening in November I learned rather more about Serena Cockayne. After working all afternoon in the study I looked up from my desk to see her sitting in the corner with her back to me. Distracted by a professional problem, I had left her there after lunch without thinking, and there was something rather melancholy about her rounded shoulders and inclined head, almost as if she had fallen from favour.

168

As I turned her towards me I noticed a small blemish on her left shoulder, perhaps a fleck of plaster from the ceiling. I tried to brush it away, but the discoloration remained. It occurred to me that the synthetic skin, probably made from some early experimental plastic, might have begun to deteriorate. Switching on a table-lamp, I examined Serena's shoulders more carefully.

Seen against the dark background of the study, the down-like nimbus that covered Serena's skin confirmed all my admiration of her maker's genius. Here and there a barely detectable unevenness, the thinnest mottling to suggest a surface capillary, rooted the illusion in the firmest realism. I had always assumed that this masterpiece of imitation flesh extended no more than two inches or so below the shoulder line of the gown, and that the rest of Serena's body consisted of wood and papier mâché.

Looking down at the angular planes of her shoulder blades, at the modest curvatures of her well-concealed breasts, I gave way to a sudden and wholly unprurient impulse. Standing behind her, I took the silver zip in my fingers and with a single movement lowered it to Serena's waist.

As I gazed at the unbroken expanse of white skin that extended to a pair of plump hips and the unmistakable hemispheres of her buttocks I realized that the manikin before me was that of a complete woman, and that its creator had lavished as much skill and art on those never-to-be-seen portions of her anatomy as on the visible ones.

The zip had stuck at the lower terminus of its oxidized track. There was something offensive about my struggling with the loosened dress of this half-naked woman. My fingers touched the skin in the small of her back, removing the dust that had accumulated over the years.

Running diagonally from spine to hip was the hairline of a substantial scar. I took it for granted that this marked an essential vent required in the construction of these models.

169

But the rows of opposing stitch-marks were all too obvious. I stood up, and for a few moments watched this partly disrobed woman with her inclined head and clasped hands, gazing placidly at the fireplace.

Careful not to damage her, I loosened the bodice of the gown. The upper curvatures of her breasts appeared, indented by the shoulder straps. Then I saw, an inch above the still-concealed left nipple, a large black mole.

I zipped up the gown and straightened it gently on her shoulders. Kneeling on the carpet in front of her, I looked closely into Serena's face, seeing the faint fissures at the apex of her mouth, the minute veins in her cheek, a childhood scar below her chin. A curious sense of revulsion and excitement came over me, as if I had taken part in a cannibalistic activity.

I knew now that the person seated on her gilt chair was no manikin but a once living woman, her peerless skin mounted and forever preserved by a master, not of the doll-maker's, but of the taxidermist's art.

At that moment I fell deeply in love with Serena Cockayne.

During the next month my infatuation with Serena had all the intensity of which a middle-aged man is capable. I abandoned my office, leaving the staff to cope for themselves, and spent all my time with Serena, tending her like the most dutiful lover. At huge expense I had a complex air-conditioning system installed in my house, of a type only employed in art museums. In the past I had moved Serena from warm room to cool without a thought to her complexion, assuming it to be made of some insensitive plastic, but I now carefully regulated the temperature and humidity, determined to preserve her forever. I rearranged the furniture throughout the house to avoid bruising her arms and shoulders as I carried her from floor to floor. In the mornings I would wake eagerly to find her at the foot of my bed, then seat her by me at the breakfast table. All day she stayed within my reach, smiling at me with an expression that almost convinced me she responded to my feelings.

My social life I gave up altogether, discontinuing my dinner parties and seeing few friends. One or two callers I admitted, but only to allay their suspicions. During our brief and meaningless conversations I would watch Serena across the sitting-room with all the excitement that an illicit affair can produce.

Christmas we celebrated alone. Given Serena's youth – at times when I caught her gazing across the room after some stray thought she seemed little more than a child – I decided to decorate the house for her in the traditional style, with a spangled tree, holly, streamers and mistletoe. Gradually I transformed the rooms into a series of arbours, from which she presided over our festivities like the madonna of a procession of altar-pieces.

At midnight on Christmas Eve I placed her in the centre of the sitting-room, and laid my presents at her/feet. For a moment her hands seemed almost to touch, as if applauding my efforts. Bending below the mistletoe above her head, I brought my lips to within that same distance from hers that separated her hands.

To all this care and devotion Serena responded like a bride. Her slim face, once so naive with its tentative smile, relaxed into the contented pose of a fulfilled young wife. After the New Year I decided to bring us out into the world again, and held the first of a few small dinner parties. My friends were glad to see us in such good humour, accepting Serena as one of themselves. I returned to my office and worked happily through the day until I set off for home, where Serena would unfailingly wait for me with the warm regard of a proud and devoted wife.

While dressing for one of these dinner parties it occurred to me that Serena alone of us was unable to change her costume. Unhappily the first signs of an excess domesticity were beginning to show themselves in a slight casualness of her personal grooming. The once elaborate coiffure had become unsettled, and the stray blonde hairs all too obviously caught the light. In the same way the immaculate make-up of her face now showed the first signs of wear and tear.

Thinking it over, I decided to call on the services of a nearby hairdressing and beauty salon. When I telephoned them they agreed instantly to send a member of their staff to my house.

And here my troubles began. The one emotion of which I had never suspected myself, and which I had never before felt for any human being, coiled around my heart.

The young man who arrived, bringing with him a miniature pantechnicon of equipment, seemed harmless enough. Although with a swarthy and powerful physique, there was something effeminate about him, and there was clearly no danger in leaving him alone with Serena.

For all his self-assurance, he seemed surprised when I first introduced him to Serena, his suave 'Good morning, madam ...' ending in a mumble. Shivering in the cool air, he gazed at her open-mouthed, clearly stunned by her beauty and calm repose. I left him to get on with it and spent the next hour working in my study, distracted now and then by a few bars from *The Barber of Seville* and *My Fair Lady* that sounded down the stairs. When he had finished I inspected his work, delighted to see that he had restored every breath of her first glory to Serena. The over-domesticated housewife had vanished, and in her place was the naive Aphrodite I had first seen in the curio shop six months earlier.

So pleased was I that I decided to call on the young man's services again, and his visits became a weekly event. Thanks to his attentions, and my own devotion to the temperature and humidity controls, Serena's complexion regained all its perfection. Even my guests commented on the remarkable bloom of her appearance. Deeply contented, I looked forward to the coming spring and the celebration of our first anniversary.

Six weeks later, while the young hairdresser was at work in Serena's sitting-room upstairs, I happened to return to my bedroom to collect a book. I could clearly hear the young man's voice, at a low pitch as if communicating some private message. I glanced through the open door. He was kneeling in front of Serena, his back to me, cosmetic pallet in one hand and paint stick in the other, gesticulating with them in a playful and mock-comical manner. Illuminated by his handiwork, Serena gazed straight into his face, her freshly painted lips almost moist with anticipation. Unmistakably, the young man was murmuring a discreet and private endearment.

During the following days I felt that my head had been seized by some kind of vice. As I tried helplessly to master the pain of that first intense jealousy, I was forced to realize that the young man was Serena's age, and that she would always have more in common with him than with me. Superficially our life continued as before – we sat together in the study when I returned from the office, I would carry Serena into the sitting-room when my friends called, and she would join us at the dining table – but I was aware that a formal note had entered our relationship. No more did Serena pass the night in my bedroom, and I noticed that for all her calm smile I no longer caught her eye as I used to.

Despite my mounting suspicions, the young hairdresser continued to make his calls. Whatever crisis through which Serena and I were passing, I was determined not to give in. During the long hour of his visits I had to fight through every second to prevent myself from rushing up the staircase. From the hall I could often hear his voice murmuring in that insinuating tone, louder now as if he were trying to incite me. When he left I could sense his contempt.

It would take me an hour before I could walk slowly up the stairs to Serena's room. Her extraordinary beauty, relit by the taper of the young man's flattery, made my anger all the greater. Unable to speak, I would pace around her like a doomed husband, aware of the subtle changes to Serena's face. Although in every way more youthful, reminding me painfully of the thirty years that separated us, her expression after each visit became fractionally less naive, like that of a young wife contemplating her first affair. A sophisticated wave now modulated the curve of blonde hair that crossed her right temple. Her lips were slimmer, her mouth stronger and more mature.

Inevitably I began an affair with another woman, the separated wife of a close friend, but I made certain that Serena knew nothing of this or of the other infidelities that followed during the next weeks. Also, pathetically, I began to drink, and in the afternoons would sit around drunkenly in my friends' empty apartments, holding long imaginary conversations with Serena in which I was both abject and aggressive. At home I began to play the dictatorial husband, leaving her all evening in her room upstairs and moodily refusing to talk to her at the dining table. All the while, through paralysed eyes I watched the young hairdresser come and go, an insolent suitor whistling as he sauntered up the stairs.

After the last of his visits came the weary denouement. I had spent the afternoon drinking alone in a deserted restaurant, watched by the patient staff. In the taxi home I had a sudden confused revelation about Serena and myself. I realized that our breakdown had been entirely my fault, that my jealousy of her harmless flirtation with the young man had magnified everything to absurd proportions.

Released from weeks of agony by this decision, I paid off

the taxi at my door, let myself into the cool air of the house and rushed upstairs. Dishevelled but happy, I walked towards Serena as she sat quietly in the centre of her sitting-room ready to embrace her and forgive us both.

Then I noticed that for all her immaculate make-up and extravagant hair her brocade gown hung strangely from her shoulders. The right strap exposed the whole of her collar-bone, and the bodice had slipped forward as if someone had been fumbling with her breast. Her smile still hovered on her lips, as if calling on me in the most kindly way to resign myself to the realities of adult life.

Angrily I stepped forward and slapped her face.

How I regret that senseless spasm. In the two years that have passed I have had ample time to reflect on the dangers of an over-hasty catharsis. Serena and I still live together, but all is over between us. She sits on her gilt chair by the sitting-room fireplace and joins me at the dining table when I entertain my friends. But the outward show of our relation-ship is nothing more than the dried husk from which the body of feeling has vanished.

At first, after that blow to her face, little seemed to change. I remember standing in that room upstairs with my bruised hand. I calmed myself, brushed the face powder from my knuckles and decided to review my life. From then on I stopped drinking and went to the office each day, devoting myself to my work.

For Serena, however, the incident marked the first stage in what proved to be a decisive transformation. Within a few days I realized that she had lost something of her bloom. Her face became drawn, her nose more protuberant. The corner of her mouth where I had struck her soon became puffy and took on a kind of ironic downward twist. In the absence of the young hairdresser – whom I had sacked within ten minutes of striking her – Serena's decline seemed to accelerate. The elaborate coiffure which the young man had foisted upon her soon became undone, the straggling hairs falling on her shoulders.

By the end of our second year together Serena Cockayne had aged a full decade. At times, looking at her hunched on her gilt chair in the still brilliant gown, I almost believed that she had set out to catch and overtake me as part of some complex scheme of revenge. Her posture had slumped, and her rounded shoulders gave her the premature stoop of an old woman. With her unfocussed smile and straggling hair she often reminded me of a tired and middle-aged spinster. Her hands had at last come together, clasped in a protective and wistful way.

Recently a far more disquieting development has taken place. Three years after our first meeting Serena entered upon a radically new stage of deterioration. As a result of some inherent spinal weakness, perhaps associated with the operation whose scars cross the small of her back, Serena's posture has altered. In the past she leaned forward slightly, but three days ago I found that she had slumped back in her chair. She sits there now in a stiff and awkward way, surveying the world with a critical and unbalanced eye, like some dotty faded beauty. One eyelid has partly closed, and gives her ashen face an almost cadaverous look. Her hands have continued on their slow collision, and have begun to twist upon each other, rotating to produce a deformed parody of themselves that will soon become an obscene gesture.

Above all, it is her smile that terrifies me. The sight of it has unsettled my entire life, but I find it impossible to move my eyes from it. As her face has sagged, the smile has become wider and even more askew. Although it has taken two years to achieve its full effect, that blow to her mouth has turned it into a reproachful grimace. There is something knowing and implacable about Serena's smile. As I look at it now across the study it seems to contain a complete understanding of my character, a judgment unknown to me from which I can never escape.

Each day the smile creeps a little further across her face. Its progress is erratic, revealing aspects of her contempt for me that leave me numb and speechless. It is cold here, as the low temperature helps to preserve Serena. By turning on the heating system I could probably dispose of her in a few weeks, but this I can never do. That smirk of hers alone prevents me. Besides, I am completely bound to Serena.

Fortunately, Serena is now ageing faster than I am. Helplessly watching her smile, my overcoat around my shoulders, I wait for her to die and set me free.

Motel Architecture

Pangborn's suspicion that someone was hiding in the solarium coincided with the arrival of the young repairwoman. The presence of this smartly uniformed but bored girl rattling her metal valise around his wheelchair so frayed his nerves that at first he made no attempt to find the intruder. Her aggressive manner, the interminable whistling she kept up as she wiped the television screens, and her growing interest in Pangborn were unlike anything he had previously had to deal with.

The uniformed women sent by the company to maintain the services within the solarium had been noted for their silence and efficiency. Looking back at the twelve years he had spent in the solarium, Pangborn could hardly recall a single face. In fact, the absence of any kind of personal identity allowed the young women to carry out their intimate chores. Yet even within the hour of her first visit this new recruit had managed to damage the tuning control of the master screen and unsettle Pangborn with her moody gaze. But for this vague and unsettling criticism of him Pangborn would have identified the intruder far earlier and avoided the strange consequences that were to follow.

At the time he had been sitting in his chair in the centre of the solarium, bathing in the warm artificial light that flowed through the ceiling vents and watching the shower sequence from *Psycho* on the master screen. The brilliance of this *tour de force* never ceased to astonish Pangborn. He had played the sequence to himself hundreds of times, frozen every frame and explored it in close-up, separately recorded sections of the action and displayed them on the dozen smaller screens around the master display. The extraordinary relationship between the geometry of the shower stall and the anatomy of the murdered woman's body seemed to hold the clue to the real meaning of everything in Pangborn's world, to the unstated connections between his own musculature and the immaculate glass and chromium universe of the solarium. In his headier moments Pangborn was convinced that the secret formulas of his tenancy of time and space were contained somewhere within this endlessly repeated clip of film.

So immersed had he been in the mysterious climax of the sequence — the slewing face of the actress pressed against the tiled floor with its rectilinear grid — that at first he ignored the faint noise of breathing nearby, the half-familiar smell of a human being.

Pangborn turned in his wheelchair, expecting to find someone standing behind him, perhaps one of the delivery men who provisioned the solarium's kitchen and fuel tanks. After twelve years of living entirely on his own, Pangborn had discovered that his senses were sharp enough to detect the presence of a single fly.

Freezing the film on the television screens, he swung his chair and turned his back to them. The circular chamber was empty, like the uncurtained bathroom and kitchen.

But the air had moved, somewhere behind him a heart had beaten, lungs had breathed.

At this moment a key turned in the entrance hall, the glass door was banged back by a clumsily carried vacuum-cleaner, and Vera Tilley made her first appearance.

For all his intimacy with the electronic image of the naked film actress, Pangborn had not looked a real woman in the face for more than ten years. Still unsettled by the suspected intruder, he watched the uniformed girl drop her vacuum-cleaner on to the carpet and root about in her tool-kit. She was barely twenty, with untidy blonde hair pushed up into her cap, eccentric make-up applied to her already large mouth and eyes. On her lapel was an identification badge – under the company's heraldic device was the name 'Vera Tilley' and a photograph of her staring at the camera with a cheeky pout.

She now gazed at Pangborn and the solarium in the same provocative way.

'When you're ready you can carry on,' Pangborn told her. 'I'm busy at the moment.'

'So I can see.' The girl eyed the complex of screens, the huge blow-ups of the dead eyes of the actress surrounded like an electronic altar-piece by the quantified sections of her body on the smaller displays. With a wry glance at Pangborn's padded contour chair, she remarked: 'Is she comfortable up there? Can't you do something for her?' She flicked a dirty finger-nail at the control console on the arm of the chair. 'You've got enough buttons to stop the world.'

Ignoring her, Pangborn rotated the chair and returned to the screens. For the next hour, as he continued his analysis of the shower sequence, he was still thinking of the intruder. Clearly there was no one hiding in the solarium now, but the presence of this mysterious visitor might in some way be connected with the odd young woman. He could almost believe that she was some new kind of urban terrorist. He listened to her moving around the kitchen, servicing the equipment and replacing the supplies in the food dispensers. Every now and then her whistling was modulated by an ironic note.

When she had cleaned the bathroom she came back and

stood between Pangborn and the screens. He could smell his cologne on her wrists.

'Time to switch off the life-support system,' she said goodhumouredly. 'Can you survive for five minutes on your own?'

Pangborn waited impatiently while she swung each of the television sets from the wall and tuned its controls. As he watched this young woman at work, kneeling in front of him on the carpet, he felt strangely vulnerable. Her breathing, her plump calves, the coarse vitality of her body, made him wish that it were possible to dispense with any need to maintain the solarium. He had been celibate for the past 15 years, and his confused feelings unsettled him. He preferred the secure realities of the television screens to the endlessly bizarre fictions of ordinary life. At the same time Vera Tilley intrigued him. He thought again of the intruder.

'See you next week,' she told him as he signed the work schedule. While she packed her valise she watched him with some concern. 'Don't you ever get tired of looking at those old films? You ought to go out once in a while. My brother owns a taxi if you ever want one.'

Pangborn waved her away, his eyes on the magnified image of the bathroom floor and the strange contours of the film actress's cheekbones. But when the door opened he called out: 'Tell me, I meant to ask – when you arrived, was there anyone waiting outside?'

'Only if he was invisible.' Puzzled by Pangborn's deliberately casual tone, she weighed the valise in her strong hand, as if about to take out her screwdriver and turn down his over-active image control. 'You're alone here, Mr Pangborn. Perhaps you saw a ghost...'

After she had gone Pangborn lay back in his chair and scanned through the afternoon's public television programmes. With her slapdash manner, the girl had mistuned the master screen, dappling everything with an intermittent interference pattern, but for once Pangborn was able to ignore this. He turned off the sound and watched the dozens of programmes move past silently.

Once again, unmistakably, he was aware of the presence of someone nearby. The faint voice of another human being hung on the air, the spoor of an unfamiliar body. There was an odd but not unpleasant odour in the solarium. Pangborn left the screens and drove the wheelchair around the chamber, inspecting the kitchen, hall and bathroom. He could see that the solarium was empty, but at the same time he was convinced that someone was watching him.

The girl, Vera Tilley, had unsettled him in a way he had not expected. All his experience, his years spent in front of the television screens, had not prepared him for even the briefest encounter with an actual woman. What would once have been called the 'real' world, the quiet streets outside, the private estate of hundreds of similar solaria, made no effort to intrude itself into Pangborn's private world and he had never felt any need to defend himself against it.

Looking down at himself, he realized that he had been naked during her visit. Bathed in the ceaseless light of the solarium, he had years ago given up wearing even his loin-slip. So distant and anonymous were the repair-women usually sent by the company that he felt no embarrassment as they moved around him.

However, Vera Tilley had made him aware of himself for the first time. No doubt she had noticed just how she had aroused him. Trying not to think of her, Pangborn stiffened the back of the chair and concentrated on the television screens in front of him. Calmed by the warm light flowing across his bronzed body, he switched off the public channels and returned to his analysis of *Psycho*. The geometry of the naked actress slumped across the floor of the shower stall provided an endless source of interest, like the most abstract possible of all music, and within a few minutes he was able to lower the back of the chair, Vera Tilley and the mysterious intruder forgotten.

During his twelve years in the solarium Pangborn had never left the light-filled chamber, and recently had hardly even left the chair. For the few minutes each day which he was forced to spend standing in the bathroom he felt strangely heavy and cumbersome, his body an uncouth mass of superfluous musculature suspended as if by a bad sculptor on the slender armature of his bones. Lying back on the chair, he found it hard to believe that the sleek, bronzed figure projected by the monitor camera on to the screens in front of him was that same shaky invalid who faced him in the bathroom mirror. As far as possible Pangborn remained in the chair, wheeling himself into the kitchen, preparing his meals sitting down, in a sense remaking a small second world within the private universe of the solarium.

This spherical chamber where he seemed to have spent his entire life, asleep and awake, by now supplied all his needs, both physical and psychological. The chamber was at once a gymnasium and bedroom, library and workplace (nominally Pangborn was a television critic, virtually the only job, apart from that of the maintenance engineers, in a society where everything else was done by machine). Mounted on the rear wall of the solarium was a cluster of exercise devices which he operated for half an hour each day while sitting in the chair.

The bathroom was also equipped with a special cabinet containing a variety of sexual appliances, but for years Pangborn had been repelled by the thought of using them – they engaged him in too unsettling a way with the facts of his own body. He felt the same resistance towards the psychological maintenance devices which everyone was encouraged to air for at least an hour each day on the television screens – simulated confrontations and reconciliations with his parents, intelligence and personality tests, and a whole range of psychological games, pocket dramas in which he could play the starring role.

183

But Pangborn had soon become bored with the limited repertory of these charades. Fantasy and the imagination had always played little part in his life, and he felt only at home within the framework of an absolute realism. The solarium was a fully equipped television studio, in which Pangborn was simultaneously the star, script-writer and director of an unending domestic serial of infinitely more interest than the programmes provided by the public channels. The news bulletins now were about his own body processes, the night's heart rate, the rising and falling curves of his temperature. These images, and the analysis of certain key events from his library of feature films, seemed to have some kind of profound though yet mysterious connection. The strange geometry presiding over the actress in her shower stall provided a key to that absolute abstraction of himself he had sought since his arrival at the solarium, the construction of a world formed entirely from the materials of his own consciousness.

During the next days Pangborn's peace of mind was interrupted by his growing awareness of the intruder who had entered the solarium. At first he put down his suspicions to Vera Tilley's arrival. The strongly scented cosmetics used by the young woman had released some repressed memory of his mother and sister, and of his brief and abortive marriage. But once again, as he lay back in his chair, analysing the ever larger blow-ups of the actress's face pressed against the bathroom tiles, he felt the presence of an uninvited visitor somewhere behind him. With the sound turned down he could hear the occasional breathing, even a sigh as this mysterious intruder seemed to weary of his secret vigil. Now and then Pangborn would hear a metallic creak behind him, the tension of a leather harness, and detect the faint smell of another body.

For once ignoring his television screens, Pangborn began

a painstaking inspection of the solarium, starting with the hall and its storage cupboards. He pulled out the racks of cassettes, the cases filled with suits he had not worn for ten years. Satisfied that the hall provided no hiding place, he drove the wheelchair into the bathroom and kitchen, searched the medicine cabinet and shower, the narrow spaces behind the refrigerator and cooker. It occurred to him that the intruder might be some small animal which had slipped into the solarium during a visit by one of the cleaners. But as he sat motionlessly in the light-filled silence he could hear the steady breathing of a human being.

By the time of Vera Tilley's second visit Pangborn was waiting at the door of the solarium. He hoped to catch a glimpse of someone loitering outside, perhaps an accomplice of the intruder. Already he suspected that they might be members of a gang hoping to rig the television audience surveys.

'You're on my foot, Mr Pangborn! What's the matter? Don't you want me to come in today?' Pushing the door against the wheelchair, Vera looked down at Pangborn. 'You're in a state.'

Pangborn reversed into the centre of the solarium. The young woman's make-up seemed less bizarre, as if she intended to reveal more of herself to him. Realizing suddenly that he was naked, he felt his skin prickle uncomfortably.

'Did you see anyone outside? Waiting in a car, or watching the door?'

'You asked me that last week.' Ignoring his agitated condition, Vera opened her tool-kit and began to fit together the sections of the vacuum-cleaner. 'Are you expecting someone to stay?'

'No!' The thought appalled Pangborn. Even the presence of the young woman exhausted him. He remembered the sounds of breathing behind the chair. Calming himself, he said: 'Leave the cleaning until later and have a look at the aerials. I think one of the sets is picking up a strange sound-track – perhaps from the studio next door.'

Pangborn waited while she worked away at the sets. Afterwards he followed her around the solarium in his wheelchair, watching as she cleaned the bathroom and kitchen. He peered between her legs into the shower stall and garbage disposal chute, confirming for himself that there was no one hiding there.

'You're all alone, Mr Pangborn. Just you and the TV screens.' As she locked her valise Vera watched him in a concerned way. 'Have you ever been to the zoo, Mr Pangborn?'

'What...? There are wild-life programmes I sometimes review.' Pangborn waited impatiently for her to leave, relieved that he could get on with his work. Watching the dozen television screens, which the girl had tuned to a needle-like sharpness, he was suddenly convinced that the notion of an intruder had all been a delusion fostered by the unsettled presence of this young woman.

However, only a few minutes after she had gone Pangborn once again heard the sounds of the intruder behind him, and the noise of the man's breathing, even louder now as if he had decided no longer to conceal his presence from Pangborn.

Controlling himself, Pangborn took stock of the solarium. An unvarying light fell through the glass vents into this world without shadows, bathing the chamber in an almost submarine glow. He had been reviewing a programme of redubbed films – a huge repertory of transcribed classics now existed, their story lines and dialogue totally unconnected with their originals. Pangborn had been watching a tinted and redubbed version of *Casablanca*, now a new instructional film in a hotel management course on the pitfalls and satisfactions of overseas nightclub operation.

186

Ignoring the trite dialogue, Pangborn was enjoying the timelessly elegant direction when a colour fault on the master screen began to turn the characters' faces green.

As he switched off the wall of screens, about to call the maintenance company, Pangborn heard the distinctive sounds of breathing. He froze in his chair, listening to the characteristic rise and fall of human respiration. As if aware that Pangborn was listening to him, the intruder began to breathe more heavily, the harsh, deep breaths of a man in fear.

Coolly, Pangborn kept his back to the intruder, who was hiding either in the hall or bathroom. He could not only hear but smell the man's fear, the vaguely familiar scent he had noticed the previous week. For some reason he was almost sure that the man had no intention of attacking him, and was only trying to escape from the solarium. Perhaps he was an exhausted fugitive from some act of mis-justice, a wrongly incarcerated mental patient.

For the rest of the afternoon Pangborn pretended to watch the defective television screens, while systematically devising a method of dealing with the intruder. First of all he needed to establish the man's identity. He switched on the monitor camera that surveyed the solarium and set it on continuous traverse across the bathroom, kitchen and hall.

Pangborn then turned to setting a number of small traps. He unlocked the medicine cabinet in the bathroom, marking the positions of the antiseptic cream and Band-aids. After a deliberately early supper he left untouched a small filet steak and a bowl of salad. He placed a fresh bar of soap in the shower tray and scattered a fine mist of talc on the bathroom carpet.

Satisfied, he returned to the television screens and lay half-awake until the small hours, listening to the faint breathing somewhere behind him as he carried out his endless analysis of the murder sequence from *Psycho*. The immaculate and soundless junction of the film actress's skin and the white bathroom tiles, magnified in a vast close-up, contained the secret formulas that somewhere united his own body to the white fabric and soft chrome of his contour couch.

When he woke the next morning he once again heard the intruder's breathing, so rested that his mysterious visitor seemed almost to be part of everyday life in the solarium. Sure enough, as Pangborn had expected, all the modest traps had been sprung. The man had washed his hands with the fresh bar of soap, a small portion of the steak and salad had been eaten, a strange footprint marked the talc in the bathroom.

Unsettled by this tangible proof that he was not alone in the solarium, Pangborn stared at the footprint. The man's foot was almost the size of his own, with the same overlarge and questing big toe. Something about this similarity brought a flush of irritation to Pangborn. He felt a sudden sense of challenge, provoked by this feeling of identity with the man.

This close involvement with the intruder was redoubled when Pangborn discovered that the man had taken a book from his shelf – the almost unobtainable text of the original dialogue of *The Third Man*, now a cautionary tale put out by the world tourist authority on the perils of the language barrier. Pangborn thumbed through the pages of the scenario, half-hoping to find a further clue to the man's identity. He carefully replaced the book on the shelf. These first hints of the intruder's nature – the shared literary tastes, the shape of his feet, the sounds of his breathing and his body smell – both intrigued and provoked him.

As he played at high speed through the hours of film the solarium camera had recorded, he now and then caught what seemed to be brief glimpses of the intruder – the flash of an elbow behind the bathroom door, a shoulder framed against the medicine cabinet, the back of a head in the hall. Pangborn gazed at these magnifications, expanding them beside the stills from *Psycho*, the systems of two parallel but coinciding geometries.

This never explicit but civilized duel between them continued during the next days. At times Pangborn felt that he was running a *ménage à deux*. He effectively cooked meals for them both – the intruder fortunately approved of Pangborn's tastes in wine, and often reinforced the night with small measures of Pangborn's brandy. Above all, their intellectual tastes coincided – their interests in film, in abstract painting, and in the architecture of large structures. Indeed, Pangborn almost visualized them openly sharing the solarium, embarking together on their rejection of the world and the exploration of their absolute selves, their unique time and space.

All the more bitter, therefore, were Pangborn's reactions when he discovered the intruder's attempt to kill him.

Too stunned to reach for the telephone and call the police, Pangborn stared at the bottle of sleeping tablets. He listened to the faint breathing somewhere behind him, lower now as if the intruder were holding his breath, waiting for Pangborn's response.

Ten minutes earlier, while drinking his morning coffee, Pangborn had at first ignored its faintly acrid flavour, presumably some new spice or preservative. But after a few more sips he had almost gagged. Carefully emptying the cup into the wash-basin, he discovered the half-dissolved remains of a dozen plastic capsules.

Pangborn reached into the medicine cabinet and opened the now empty bottle of sleeping tablets. He listened to the faint breathing in the solarium. At some point, while his back was turned, the intruder had slipped the entire contents into his coffee.

He forced himself to vomit into the basin, but still felt queasy when Vera arrived an hour later.

189

'You look fed up,' she told him cheerfully. She nodded at the books scattered around the place. 'I can see you've been reading again.'

'I'm lending some books to a friend,' Pangborn reversed his chair away from her as she ambled around the chamber with her valise. Under the seat of his chair he held the handle of a vegetable knife. Looking up at the girl's over-bright make-up and guileless eyes it was hard to believe that she might be in collusion with the intruder. At the same time he was surprised that she could not hear the obvious sounds of the man's breathing. Once again Pangborn was amazed by his nimbleness, his ability to move from one end of the solarium to the other without leaving more than a few fragments of his presence on the monitor film. He assumed that the man had found a secure hiding-place, perhaps in a service shaft unknown to Pangborn.

'Mr Pangborn! Are you awake?'

With an effort, Pangborn rallied himself. He looked up to find Vera kneeling in front of him. She had pushed back her cap and was shaking his knees. He searched for the knife handle.

'Mr Pangborn – all those pills in the bathroom. What are they doing?'

Pangborn gestured vaguely. Concerned only to find a weapon, he had forgotten to wash away the capsules.

'I dropped the bottle in the basin – be careful you don't cut your hands.'

'Mr Pangborn – ' Confused, Vera stood up and straightened her cap. She glanced disapprovingly at the huge blow-ups from *Psycho* on the television screens, and at the blurred fragments of shoulder and elbow recorded by the solarium camera. 'It's like a jig-saw. Who is it? You?'

'Someone else – a friend who's been visiting me.'

'I thought so – the place is in a mess. The kitchen … Have you ever thought of getting married, Mr Pangborn?'

He stared at her, aware that she was deliberately being

coquettish, trying to unsettle him for his own sake. Once again his skin began to scream.

'You ought to get out of here more,' she was telling him sensibly. 'Visit your friend. Do you want me to come tomorrow? It's on my route. I can say your aerials need tuning.'

Pangborn reversed around her, keeping an eye on the bathroom and kitchen. Vera hesitated before leaving, searching for an excuse to prolong her stay. Pangborn was certain that this amiable scatter-brain was not an accomplice of the intruder, but if he once divulged the man's presence, let alone the murder attempt, she would probably panic and then provoke an openly homicidal assault.

Controlling his temper, he waited until she left. But any irritation he felt was soon forgotten when a second attempt was made on his life.

As with the first murder attempt, Pangborn noticed that the method chosen was both devious and clumsy. Whether because he was still half-doped by the sleeping pills, or out of sheer physical bravado, he felt no sense of panic, but only a calm determination to beat the intruder at his own game. A complex duel was taking place between them, its fragmentary course displayed in a lengthening series of giant blow-ups on the screens – his own suspicious hands a few feet from the camera, the intruder's angular shoulder silhouetted against the kitchen door, even a portion of an ear reflected in the mirror of the medicine cabinet. As Pangborn sat in his chair, comparing sections of this visual jig-saw with the elements from the shower sequence in *Psycho*, he knew that sooner or later he would assemble a complete picture of the intruder.

Meanwhile, the man's presence became ever more evident. The smell of his body filled the solarium and stained the towels in the bathroom. He openly helped himself to the food in the refrigerator, scattering shreds of salad on the floor. Tirelessly, Pangborn maintained his round-the-clock surveillance, trying to shake off the effects of the sleeping pills. So determined was he to defeat the intruder that he took for granted that the water in the bathroom tank had been fouled with cleaning soda. Later, in the kitchen, as he bathed his stinging face with mineral water, he could hear the self-satisfied breathing of the intruder, celebrating another small deceit.

Later that night, as he lay half-asleep in front of the television screens, he woke with a start to feel the hot breath of the stranger against his face. Startled, he looked round in the flickering light to find the vegetable knife on the carpet and a small wound on his right knee.

For the first time a foul smell pervaded the solarium, an unpleasant blend of disinfectant, excrement, and physical rage, like the atmosphere of some ill-maintained psychiatric institution.

Retching on to the carpet beside his chair, Pangborn turned his back to the television screens. Holding the vegetable knife in front of him, he headed for the hall. He unlocked the front door, waiting for the cool night air to invade the solarium. Leaving the door ajar, he wheeled himself to the telephone beside the screens.

As he held the severed flex in his hands he heard the hall door close quietly. So the intruder had decided to leave, resigning from their duel even though Pangborn was now unable to contact the outside world.

Pangborn looked at the screens, regretting that he would never complete the jig-saw. The foul smell still hung on the air, and Pangborn decided to take a shower before going out to use a neighbour's telephone.

But as he entered the bathroom he could see clearly the bloody rents in the shower curtain. Pulling it back, he recognized the body of the young repair-woman, lying face down on the tiled floor, and the familiar postures he had analysed in a thousand blow-ups.

Appalled by the calm expression in Vera's eyes, as if she had known full well the role in which she had been cast, Pangborn reversed his chair into the solarium. He gripped the knife, feeling her wounds in the pain in his leg, and aware once again of the deep breathing around him.

Everything now, in this final phase, was in close-up. After recording the position of the girl's body with his portable camera — the film would be vital evidence for the investigating police — Pangborn sat in front of the wall of screens. He was certain that the last confrontation was about to take place between himself and the intruder. Holding the knife in his hand, he waited for the attack to come. The sounds in the solarium seemed amplified, and he could hear the intruder's pumping lungs and feel his frightened pulse drumming through the floor into the arms of his chair.

Pangborn waited for him to come, his eyes on the screen, the monitor camera focussed directly upon himself. He watched the huge close-ups of his own body, of the film actress on the floor of her bathroom, and of Vera's sprawled form entangled with the white shower curtains. As he adjusted the controls, moving these areas of tile and flesh into ever-closer focus, Pangborn felt himself rising beyond anger into an almost sexual lust for the intruder's death, the first erotic impulse he had known since he had begun watching these television screens so many years earlier. The smell of the man's body, the beat of his pulse and hot breath seemed to be moving towards an orgasmic climax. Their collision when it came in the next few minutes would be an act of intercourse, which would at last provide the key he needed.

Pangborn held the knife, watching the whitening screens, anonymous rectangles of blank skin that formed a fragmented sky. Somewhere among them the elements of the human form still remained, a residual nexus of contour and texture in which Pangborn could at last perceive the unmistakable outline of the stranger's face.

Eyes fixed upon the screens, he waited for the man to touch him, certain that he had mesmerized the intruder with these obsessive images. He felt no hostility towards the man, and was aware now that over the years in the solarium he had become so detached from external reality that even he himself had become a stranger. The odours and sounds that disgusted him were those of his own body. All along, the intruder in the solarium had been himself. In his search for absolute peace he had found one last limiting obstacle – the intrusive fact of his own consciousness. Without this, he would merge forever into the universe of the infinite close-up. He was sorry for the young woman, but it was she who had first provoked him into his disgust with himself.

Eager now to merge with the white sky of the screen, to find that death in which he would be rid forever of himself, of his intruding mind and body, he raised the knife to his happy heart.

The Intensive Care Unit

Within a few minutes the next attack will begin. Now that I am surrounded for the first time by all the members of my family it seems only fitting that a complete record should be made of this unique event. As I lie here – barely able to breathe, my mouth filled with blood and every tremor of my hands reflected in the attentive eye of the camera six feet away – I realize that there are many who will think my choice of subject a curious one. In all senses, this film will be the ultimate home-movie, and I only hope that whoever watches it will gain some idea of the immense affection I feel for my wife, and for my son and daughter, and of the affection that they, in their unique way, feel for me.

It is now half an hour since the explosion, and everything in this once elegant sitting-room is silent. I am lying on the floor by the settee, looking at the camera mounted safely out of reach on the ceiling above my head. In this uneasy stillness, broken only by my wife's faint breathing and the irregular movement of my son across the carpet, I can see that almost everything I have assembled so lovingly during the past years has been destroyed. My Sèvres lies in a thousand fragments in the fireplace, the Hokusai scrolls are punctured in a dozen places. Yet despite the extensive damage this is still recognizably the scene of a family reunion, though of a rather special kind.

My son David crouches at his mother's feet, chin resting on the torn Persian carpet, his slow movement marked by a series of smeared hand-prints. Now and then, when he raises his head, I can see that he is still alive. His eyes are watching me, calculating the distance between us and the time it will take him to reach me. His sister Karen is little more than an arm's length away, lying beside the fallen standard lamp between the settee and the fireplace, but he ignores her. Despite my fear, I feel a powerful sense of pride that he should have left his mother and set out on this immense journey towards me. For his own sake I would rather he lay still and conserved what little strength and time are left to him, but he presses on with all the determination his seven-year-old body can muster.

My wife Margaret, who is sitting in the armchair facing me, raises her hand in some kind of confused warning, and then lets it fall limply on to the stained damask arm-rest. Distorted by her smudged lipstick, the brief smile she gives me might seem to the casual spectator of this film to be ironic or even threatening, but I am merely struck once again by her remarkable beauty. Watching her, and relieved that she will probably never rise from her armchair again, I think of our first meeting ten years ago, then as now within the benevolent gaze of the television camera.

The unusual, not to say illicit, notion of actually meeting my wife and children in the flesh had occurred to me some three months earlier, during one of our extended family breakfasts. Since the earliest days of our marriage Sunday mornings had always been especially enjoyable. There were the pleasures of breakfast in bed, of talking over the papers and whatever else had taken place during the week. Switching to our private channel, Margaret and I would make love, celebrating the deep peace of our marriage beds. Later, we would call in the children and watch them playing in their nurseries, and perhaps surprise them with the promise of a visit to the park or circus.

196

All these activities, of course, like our family life itself, were made possible by television. At that time neither I nor anyone else had ever dreamed that we might actually meet in person. In fact, age-old though rarely invoked ordinances still existed to prevent this – to meet another human being was an indictable offence (especially, for reasons I then failed to understand, a member of one's own family, presumably part of some ancient system of incest taboos). My own upbringing, my education and medical practice, my courtship of Margaret and our happy marriage, all occurred within the generous rectangle of the television screen. Margaret's insemination was of course by AID, and like all children David's and Karen's only contact with their mother was during their brief uterine life.

In every sense, needless to say, this brought about an immense increase in the richness of human experience. As a child I had been brought up in the hospital crèche, and thus spared all the psychological dangers of a physically intimate family life (not to mention the hazards, aesthetic and otherwise, of a shared domestic hygiene). But far from being isolated I was surrounded by companions. On television I was never alone. In my nursery I played hours of happy games with my parents, who watched me from the comfort of their homes, feeding on to my screen a host of video-games, animated cartoons, wild-life films and family serials which together opened the world to me.

My five years as a medical student passed without my ever needing to see a patient in the flesh. My skills in anatomy and physiology were learned at the computer display terminal. Advanced techniques of diagnosis and surgery eliminated any need for direct contact with an organic illness. The probing camera, with its infra-red and X-ray scanners, its computerized diagnostic aids, revealed far more than any unaided human eye.

Perhaps I was especially adept at handling these complex keyboards and retrieval systems – a finger-tip sensitivity that was the modern equivalent of the classical surgeon's operative skills – but by the age of thirty I had already established a thriving general practice. Freed from the need to visit my surgery in person, my patients would merely dial themselves on to my television screen. The selection of these incoming calls – how tactfully to fade out a menopausal housewife and cut to a dysenteric child, while remembering to cue in separately the anxious parents – required a considerable degree of skill, particularly as the patients themselves shared these talents. The more neurotic patients usually far exceeded them, presenting themselves with the disjointed cutting, aggressive zooms and split-screen techniques that went far beyond the worst excesses of experimental cinema.

My first meeting with Margaret took place when she called me during a busy morning surgery. As I glanced into what was still known nostalgically as 'the waiting room' – the visual display projecting brief filmic profiles of the day's patients – I would customarily have postponed to the next day any patient calling without an appointment. But I was immediately struck, first by her age – she seemed to be in her late twenties – and then by the remarkable pallor of this young woman. Below close-cropped blonde hair her underlit eyes and slim mouth were set in a face that was almost ashen. I realized that, unlike myself and everyone else, she was wearing no make-up for the cameras. This accounted both for her arctic skin-tones and for her youthless appearance – on television, thanks to make-up, everyone of whatever age was 22, the cruel divisions of chronology banished for good.

It must have been this absence of make-up that first seeded the idea, to flower with such devastating consequences ten years later, of actually meeting Margaret in person. Intrigued by her unclassifiable appearance, I shelved my other patients and began our interview. She told me that she was a masseuse, and after a polite preamble came to the point. For some months she had been concerned that a small lump in her left breast might be cancerous.

I made some reassuring reply, and told her that I would examine her. At this point, without warning, she leaned forward, unbuttoned her shirt and exposed her breast.

Startled, I stared at this huge organ, some two feet in diameter, which filled my television screen. An almost Victorian code of visual ethics governed the doctor/patient relationship, as it did all social intercourse. No physician ever saw his patients undressed, and the location of any intimate ailments was always indicated by the patient by means of diagram slides. Even among married couples the partial exposure of their bodies was a comparative rarity, and the sexual organs usually remained veiled behind the most misty filters, or were coyly alluded to by the exchange of cartoon drawings. Of course, a clandestine pornographic channel operated, and prostitutes of both sexes plied their wares, but even the most expensive of these would never appear live, instead substituting a pre-recorded film-strip of themselves at the moment of climax.

These admirable conventions eliminated all the dangers of personal involvement, and this liberating affectlessness allowed those who so wished to explore the fullest range of sexual possibility and paved the way for the day when a truly guilt-free sexual perversity and, even, psychopathology might be enjoyed by all.

Staring at the vast breast and nipple, with their uncompromising geometries, I decided that my best way of dealing with this eccentrically frank young woman was to ignore any lapse from convention. After the infra-red examination confirmed that the suspected cancer nodule was in fact a benign cyst she buttoned her shirt and said:

'That's a relief. Do call me, doctor, if you ever need a course of massage. I'll be delighted to repay you.'

Though still intrigued by her, I was about to roll the credits at the conclusion of this bizarre consultation when

199

her casual offer lodged in my mind. Curious to see her again, I arranged an appointment for the following week.

Without realizing it, I had already begun my courtship of this unusual young woman. On the evening of my appointment, I half-suspected that she was some kind of novice prostitute. However, as I lay discreetly robed on the recreation couch in my sauna, manipulating my body in response to Margaret's instructions, there was not the slightest hint of salaciousness. During the evenings that followed I never once detected a glimmer of sexual awareness, though at times, as we moved through our exercises together, we revealed far more of our bodies to each other than many married couples. Margaret, I realized, was a sport, one of those rare people with no sense of self-consciousness, and little awareness of the prurient emotions she might arouse in others.

Our courtship entered a more formal phase. We began to go out together – that is, we shared the same films on television, visited the same theatres and concert halls, watched the same meals prepared in restaurants, all within the comfort of our respective homes. In fact, at this time I had no idea where Margaret lived, whether she was five miles away from me or five hundred. Shyly at first, we exchanged old footage of ourselves, of our childhoods and schooldays, our favourite foreign resorts.

Six months later we were married, at a lavish ceremony in the most exclusive of the studio chapels. Over two hundred guests attended, joining a huge hook-up of television screens, and the service was conducted by a priest renowned for his mastery of the split-screen technique. Pre-recorded films of Margaret and myself taken separately in our own sitting-rooms were projected against a cathedral interior and showed us walking together down an immense aisle.

For our honeymoon we went to Venice. Happily we shared the panoramic views of the crowds in St Mark's Square, and gazed at the Tintorettos in the Academy

School. Our wedding night was a triumph of the director's art. As we lay in our respective beds (Margaret was in fact some thirty miles to the south of me, somewhere in a complex of vast high-rises), I courted Margaret with a series of increasingly bold zooms, which she countered in a sweetly teasing way with her shy fades and wipes. As we undressed and exposed ourselves to each other the screens merged into a last oblivious close-up...

From the start we made a handsome couple, sharing all our interests, spending more time on the screen together than any couple we knew. In due course, through AID, Karen was conceived and born, and soon after her second birthday in the residential crèche she was joined by David.

Seven further years followed of domestic bliss. During this period I had made an impressive reputation for myself as a paediatrician of advanced views by my championship of family life – this fundamental unit, as I described it, of intensive care. I repeatedly urged the installation of more cameras throughout the homes of family members, and provoked vigorous controversy when I suggested that families should bathe together, move naked but without embarrassment around their respective bedrooms, and even that fathers should attend (though not in close-up) the births of their children.

It was during a pleasant family breakfast together that there occurred to me the extraordinary idea that was so dramatically to change our lives. I was looking at the image of Margaret on the screen, enjoying the beauty of the cosmetic mask she now wore – ever thicker and more elaborate as the years passed, it made her grow younger all the time. I relished the elegantly stylized way in which we now presented ourselves to each other – fortunately we had moved from the earnestness of Bergman and the more facile mannerisms of Fellini and Hitchcock to the classical

201

serenity and wit of René Clair and Max Ophuls, though the children, with their love of the hand-held camera, still resembled so many budding Godards.

Recalling the abrupt way in which Margaret had first revealed herself to me, I realized that the logical extension of Margaret's frankness – on which, effectively, I had built my career – was that we should all meet together in person. Throughout my entire life, I reflected, I had never once seen, let alone touched, another human being. Whom better to begin with than my own wife and children?

Tentatively I raised the suggestion with Margaret, and I was delighted when she agreed.

'What an odd but marvellous idea! Why on earth has no one suggested it before?'

We decided instantly that the archaic interdiction against meeting another human being deserved simply to be ignored.

Unhappily, for reasons I failed to understand at the time, our first meeting was not a success. To avoid confusing the children, we deliberately restricted the first encounter to ourselves. I remember the days of anticipation as we made preparations for Margaret's journey – an elaborate undertaking, for people rarely travelled, except at the speed of the television signal.

An hour before she arrived I disconnected the complex security precautions that sealed my house from the world outside, the electronic alarm signals, steel grilles and gastight doors.

At last the bell rang. Standing by the internal portcullis at the end of the entrance hall, I released the magnetic catches on the front door. A few seconds later the figure of a small, narrow-shouldered woman stepped into the hall. Although she was over twenty feet from me I could see her clearly, but I almost failed to realize that this was the wife to whom I had been married for ten years.

Neither of us was wearing make-up. Without its cosmetic mask Margaret's face seemed pasty and unhealthy, and the movements of her white hands were nervous and unsettled. I was struck by her advanced age and, above all, by her small size. For years I had known Margaret as a huge close-up on one or other of the large television screens in the house. Even in long-shot she was usually larger than this hunched and diminutive woman hovering at the end of the hall. It was difficult to believe that I had ever been excited by her empty breasts and narrow thighs.

Embarrassed by each other, we stood without speaking at opposite ends of the hall. I knew from her expression that Margaret was as surprised by my appearance as I was by her own. In addition, there was a curiously searching look in her eye, an element almost of hostility that I had never seen before.

Without thinking, I moved my hand to the latch of the portcullis. Already Margaret had stepped back into the doorway, as if nervous that I might seal her into the hall forever. Before I could speak, she had turned and fled.

When she had gone I carefully checked the locks on the front door. Around the entrance hung a faint and not altogether pleasant odour.

After this first abortive meeting Margaret and I returned to the happy peace of our married life. So relieved was I to see her on the screen that I could hardly believe our meeting had ever taken place. Neither of us referred to the disaster, and to the unpleasant emotions which our brief encounter had prompted.

During the next few days I reflected painfully on the experience. Far from bringing us together, the meeting had separated us. True closeness, I now knew, was television closeness – the intimacy of the zoom lens, the throat microphone, the close-up itself. On the television screen there were no body odours or strained breathing, no pupil contractions and facial reflexes, no mutual sizing up of emotions and advantage, no distrust and insecurity. Affection and compassion demanded distance. Only at a distance could one find that true closeness to another human being which, with grace, might transform itself into love.

Nevertheless, we inevitably arranged a second meeting. Why we did so I have still not understood, but both of us seemed to be impelled by those very motives of curiosity and distrust that I assumed we most feared. Calmly discussing everything with Margaret, I learned that she had felt the same distaste for me that I in turn had felt for her, the same obscure hostility.

We decided that we would bring the children to our next meeting, and that we would all wear make-up, modelling our behaviour as closely as possible on our screen life together. Accordingly, three months later, Margaret and myself, David and Karen, that unit of intensive care, came together for the first time in my sitting-room.

Karen is stirring. She has rolled across the shaft of the broken standard lamp and her body faces me across the blood-stained carpet, as naked as when she stripped in front of me. This provocative act, presumably intended to jolt some incestuous fantasy buried in her father's mind, first set off the explosion of violence which has left us bloody and exhausted in the ruins of my sitting-room. For all the wounds on her body, the bruises that disfigure her small breasts, she reminds me of Manet's *Olympia*, perhaps painted a few hours after the visit of some psychotic client.

Margaret, too, is watching her daughter. She sits forward, eyeing Karen with a gaze that is both possessive and menacing. Apart from a brief lunge at my testicles, she has ignored me. For some reason the two women have selected each other as their chief targets, just as David has vented almost all his hostility on me. I had not expected the scissors to be in his hand when I first slapped him. He is only a few feet from me now, ready to mount his last assault. For some reason he seemed particularly outraged by the display of teddy bears I had mounted so carefully for him, and shreds of these dismembered animals lie everywhere on the floor.

Fortunately I can breathe a little more freely now. I move my head to take in the ceiling camera and my fellow combatants. Together we present a grotesque aspect. The heavy television make-up we all decided to wear has dissolved into a set of bizarre halloween masks.

All the same, we are at last together, and my affection for them overrides these small problems of mutual adjustment. As soon as they arrived, the bruise on my son's head and my wife's bleeding ears betrayed the evidence of some potentially lethal scuffle. I knew that it would be a testing time. But at least we are making a start, in our small way establishing the possibility of a new kind of family life.

Everyone is breathing more strongly, and the attack will clearly begin within a minute. I can see the bloody scissors in my son's hand, and remember the pain as he stabbed me. I brace myself against the settee, ready to kick his face. With my right arm I am probably strong enough to take on whoever survives the last confrontation between my wife and daughter. Smiling at them affectionately, rage thickening the blood in my throat, I am only aware of my feelings of unbounded love.